MATE HUNT

THROWN TO THE WOLVES

LOLA GLASS

Copyright © 2022 Lola Glass
authorlolaglass.com
All rights reserved. This book or any portion thereof may not be reproduced or used in any manner whatsoever without the express written permission of the author except for the use of brief quotations in a book review.
Any references to historical events, real people, or real places are used fictitiously. Names, characters, and places are products of the author's imagination.

Cover by Sanja Gombar
https://bookcoverforyou.com/

To adventure, excitement, and the unknown

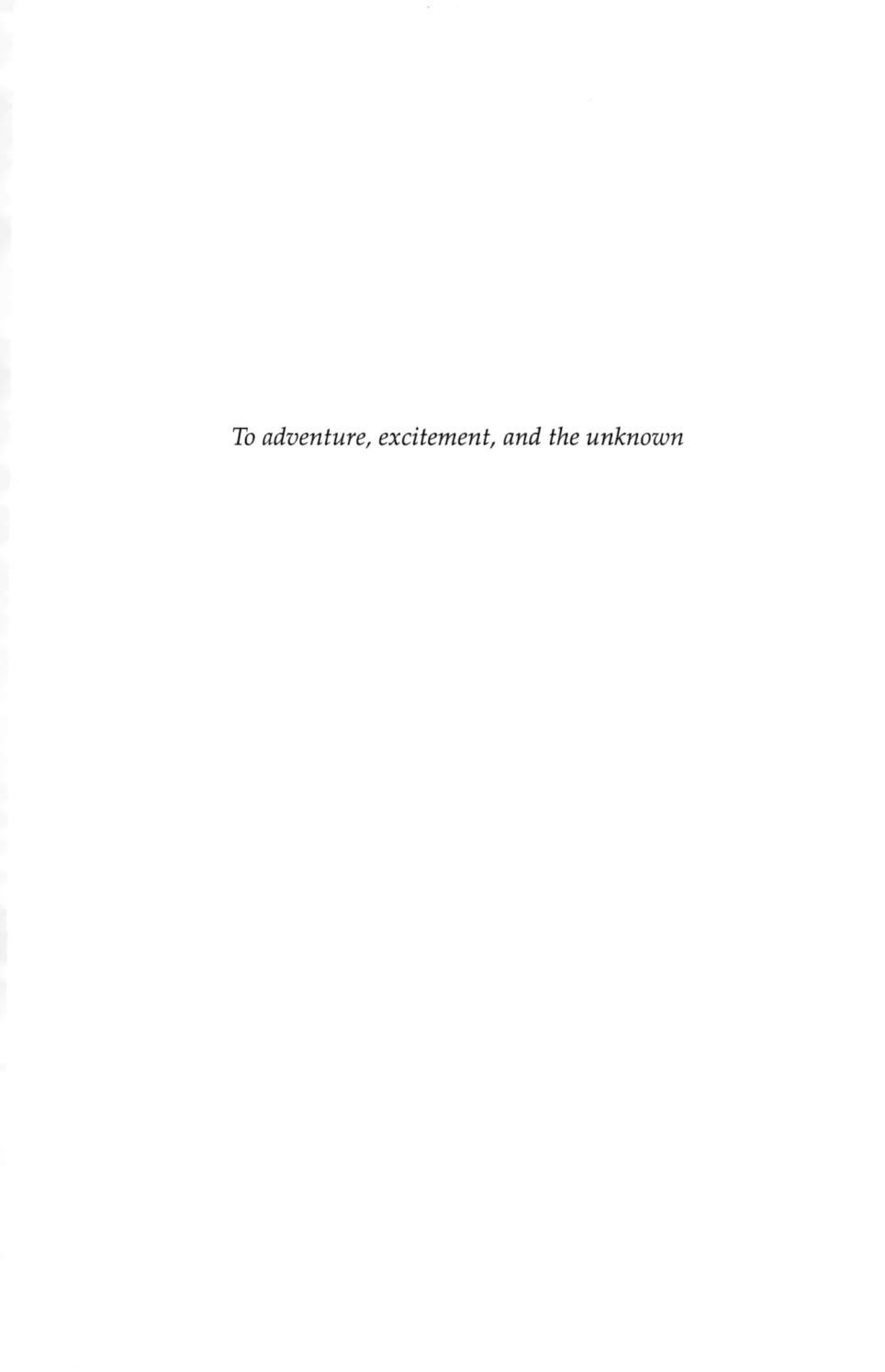

ONE

"DOUBLE THE CHEESE, triple the meat, and throw in some more of those little yellow goodies." The guy tapped his finger against the glass separating him from the line of sandwich ingredients.

The build-your-own sandwich shop I worked at was unusually busy for a Tuesday evening just before closing time. All of my classes at the nearby college were Monday/Wednesday/Friday though, so it wasn't like I had anywhere to be.

"Are you talking about the banana peppers?" I checked.

Little yellow goodies? Where did he come up with that?

They looked more green than yellow, and the sign on the glass clearly stated their name.

"The pepperoncinis." The guy's friend tapped the glass where the first had tapped.

"Those are definitely banana peppers." I added more to the sandwich before sliding down the counter and adding the ridiculous amount of mayo, oils, vinegar, and seasoning the guy wanted.

I was in the zone, barely looking away from my sandwiches long enough to call out to the rest of the customers that I'd be with them shortly.

"We'll all be paying together." A guy a little way down the line called out.

Well, that would make things easier... but also harder.

I finally looked around the sandwich shop, and my eyebrows shot upward.

Holy... had the college's entire football team come in for sandwiches or something?

The room was full of unusually tall, muscular, and attractive men. We were supposed to be closing in ten minutes, but there were at least a dozen of the guys—maybe more.

"Great." I forced a smile, tapping the buttons on the checkout screen a bit harder than I needed to.

I'd never much liked the gorgeous, muscular, popular type. Nerdy, sweet guys? They were my jam. The less ego, the better. If I ever settled down, I wanted a guy who was nice to talk to, not just look at.

I put the first guy's order in, then went back to the beginning and started his friend's sandwich.

Double cheese, triple meat.

The pattern continued with little variety as closing time passed and I continued working through the last few sandwiches. I was reaching for yet another slice of our thickest, cheesiest bread, when the last guy said,

"Veggie sandwich on flatbread."

I glanced up, surprised. The other guys hooted and cackled, tossing jokes.

"Just kidding." Veggie Guy wore a big grin. He was yet another tall, gorgeous dude who undoubtedly spent way too many hours at the gym to have many brain cells at all.

When our eyes collided, his *changed*—going from a dark green color to *red*.

I dropped the cheesy bread, scrambling backward.

The laughter died down as Veggie Guy's lips parted, and something that sounded like an animal's snarl met my ears.

"Aw, shit," one of the other guys muttered.

Veggie Guy's hand landed on the top of the glass separating us. I took a step back. When he began to move, I knew I had to go too.

I took off into the back area. There was a break room, a fridge, and a door out. I was absolutely not prepared for an emergency situation, so I booked it straight through the back door. I didn't have a car—couldn't afford the vehicle, or insurance for it—so I rushed in the direction of my dorm room.

Only a few steps down the sidewalk, a hand caught my bicep, spinning me around. I crashed into Veggie Guy and found his eyes still glowing red.

The rest of the guys caught us almost as fast. Without the glass between them and me, they looked even bigger.

"Let go of me or I'm calling the cops," I threatened, trying to look larger than I was.

Red-eyed Veggie Guy growled, low and deep. Like an animal. It sounded like he was trying to say *date*.

Wait, no. He was trying to say *mate*.

Mate? Wasn't that a British or Australian word for friend?

I really wasn't as up to date on slang from across the world as I should've been.

Suddenly, he released my arm, jerking backward and bending in half with a sharp snapping sound and a pained yell-howl. I tried to jump away from him, but my back slammed into the chest of another man.

"Grab Jesse and the girl. We need to move," the guy now holding onto me barked.

My shocked brain processed too slowly.

He threw me over his shoulder, jogging all eight steps back to the parking lot—and the lone big white kidnapper van parked outside the sandwich shop. I shouted for help as I fought to get free, but it was eleven at night and no one except the not-football-team was around.

The guy opened the door with one hand before he set me on the middle seat, then buckled me in and turned to help the other guys. I unclicked the buckle and lunged toward the door.

The guy caught me around the waist and dragged me back, buckling the belt again and holding it in place.

"You don't want to run right now," he warned, like he was on my side.

"Like hell I don't!" I ripped against the seatbelt, but he wasn't fazed and it didn't budge.

Animalistic groans, growls, and whines came from the back seat. I shuddered at the sound of cracking bones. My entire focus was on escaping, so I didn't look backward—didn't *want* to look backward.

"Drive," another guy commanded.

Someone hit the gas, and I slammed into the seatbelt hard enough to be glad I was wearing it as the van ripped around a corner.

A savage snarl met my ears, and I finally stopped fighting long enough to whirl around—

And what I saw made me want to vomit.

Veggie Guy—Mate Guy—was half human, half...animal?

Gray fur sprouted from his oddly-shaped limbs, those freaky red eyes staring at me as his body bent and contorted in another painful-sounding snap.

My voice shook as I asked, "What the hell are you?"

The guy holding the seatbelt answered with a grimace, "Werewolves."

TWO

"WHY DID YOU TAKE ME?" My heart pounded, watching the guy in the back with laser focus as his body continued to change. The van was still flying down the road, but a car crash was the least of my worries considering I'd been taken by *werewolves*.

I'd have loved to deny it, but I heard the animal-growl in Veggie Guy's voice when he grabbed me. And now, I was *watching* him turn slowly and painfully from animal to human.

"You're his mate. When a wolf finds his mate, he goes wolf and hunts until she's his," Seatbelt Guy explained quickly. "Staying with him will buy you more time."

That second part was kidnapper bullshit, for sure.

"Why would staying with a 'hunting' werewolf ever buy me *more* time?"

"Because he's going to be stuck in his wolf form until he's either changed you into one of us, or killed you. You're the she-wolf he wants, and he won't back down until you're his. He'll try to get you to offer yourself first, to ask him to change you—but there's no telling how long he'll wait, and then he's going to bite you. Werewolf venom changes the strong and kills the weak."

Well, if it killed the weak, I was in trouble. I hadn't exercised in months.

Wait, no.

It had been an entire year.

The last time I'd attempted to visit the gym was the day before classes started my freshman year, and I was currently a few weeks into my sophomore year.

"Staying with him will prolong his hunting, giving me more time before he starts biting?" I checked, still 100% planning on running as soon as I had the chance.

"Yes. It will make him feel like he's winning," Seatbelt Guy confirmed.

The van took another turn, harder and faster. My head smashed into the window, and a savage snarl broke out from Veggie Guy, who now looked almost entirely like Veggie *Wolf.*

"Shit! Sorry." Seatbelt Guy held a hand out toward the wolf in the back of the van. "Trying to keep her safe and get her away from the humans isn't easy, Jesse."

Veggie Wolf twisted his already-freaky face and made a menacing sound.

"We'll be back soon," another guy in the back with Jesse (AKA Mate-Guy-slash-Veggie-Wolf) snapped at him.

But being *back soon* was good.

It was good for me at least, because it meant that their place wasn't insanely far from mine. Which gave me at least a tiny sliver of a chance at escape.

The van turned sharply, and I slammed against the seatbelt hard enough to bruise my chest. The sudden pain made me scream. My honey-colored ponytail smacked me and Seatbelt Guy in the face as the van's tires squealed, and the floor started to sort of vibrate beneath us.

Crap. We were on a dirt road.

That was not a good thing as far as my chance of escape went. Dirt roads and I were not well acquainted.

Hell, *nature* and I weren't well acquainted.

"Faster!" someone behind me yelled.

Faster? Were they completely out of their minds?

"She's got to stop screaming or he's going to kill one of us," another guy snarled from somewhere in the van.

I screamed again, this time in hopes that he really *would* kill someone to give me a chance to get the hell away from them.

"Brakes, now," another guy barked.

The driver slammed on the brakes, no question asked. The van squealed and swerved as it skidded to a stop. There were five other guys in there with me—six if you counted Jesse's newly-furry ass—so half the group must've stayed at the sandwich shop.

All five of the non-furries bailed the second the van stopped. The doors opened and closed in record time, leaving me trapped with a wolf.

I shoved on the seatbelt, pressing and pulling and tugging, but the damn thing was stuck.

A hairy monster jumped over the seat, landing beside me on the bench. I opened my mouth to scream again.

Before I got the sound out, the monster—okay, maybe it was a wolf—shoved his head toward mine and legitimately climbed on my lap.

"You're not a dog," I yelled at it.

It licked my face.

"Not a dog," I repeated, my voice faltering a little.

It barked.

"Not a... What am I doing? I'm losing my damn mind. Get off me!" I shoved his furry body. I'd expected a werewolf to be gigantic, but he wasn't. He was only a little bigger than my mom's German Shephard, Gallifrey.

I wiggled and jiggled the seatbelt while the wolf watched me.

When I decided that wasn't going to work, I huffed and leaned back against the seat I'd been trapped in.

The wolf gave me a look, almost like it was asking, "are you done?"

I gestured toward the seatbelt, still scared out of my mind but growing angrier by the minute. "Don't just sit there, dammit. Help me!"

The wolf slashed his claws at the seatbelt. They sliced right through, and the seatbelt flew up toward the spinning mechanism.

The claw-slash reminded me what the guy had said about the wolf.

He was *hunting* me, and wouldn't stop until he'd bitten me.

And changed me into one of them.

"Stay back," I warned, scooting out of the seat and toward the door.

The wolf surprised me by *listening*.

Moving at snail speed, I slowly lifted my hand behind me, to the door's handle. When he made no move to attack, I pulled. The door clicked as it opened, and my body tensed, waiting for him to make a move.

He didn't.

The wolf just sat there, watching.

"I am so confused," I mumbled.

But when he still didn't attack me, I slowly opened the door up.

"No sudden movements," I said softly, partly to myself and partly to the wolf, because it seemed like he was *listening to me*. If he was, I would definitely take advantage of it.

I lowered one foot out of the door, poking around with the toe of my old red Converse until my foot met the dirt.

The wolf stayed where he was, watching me silently.

I slowly straightened, my hands landing on the faded fabric of the seat as I carefully lowered my second foot to the dirt.

"What's she doing?" someone whispered. One of the non-furry guys from the van, I assumed.

"I think she's trying to escape," another said, with some amusement.

"He hasn't tried to stop her yet," a third pointed out.

"He doesn't want her scared of him," a fourth responded.

Dammit, if they kept talking, all the football-player-shaped werewolves were going to be the death of me.

I took a step backward, then paused.

The wolf didn't budge.

Another step.

Pause.

No movement from Veggie Wolf.

I continued to move away from the van step-by-step, never taking my eyes off him.

Though I wasn't sure exactly which direction my dorm was, we hadn't gone far on the dirt road when the guys pulled the van over. If I ran beside it, I hoped I could get back to the real road and possibly make my way back into town.

And from there, get home.

My tiny dorm room sounded like heaven.

Right when I started to think the wolf was actually going to let me go, he jumped out of the van in one smooth, powerful movement.

Another scream welled in my throat.

Instead of letting it free, I sprinted down the dirt road.

THREE

THE WOLF CAUGHT me in less than three seconds, but he didn't tackle me or anything. He simply ran beside me.

It was so dark that I had a hard time staying on the road. But the sides of the road were sort of raised, so as long as I stuck to one of the raised edges, I knew I could make it.

I didn't stop. It was dark, so I could barely see a thing. My lungs burned, sweat poured off me, and I panted like I was the wild animal instead of him as we ran.

The wolf was nearly silent, remaining steadily beside me even as my jogging slowed to walking. My legs shook like Jell-O as I wheezed, trying hard to keep going.

When I couldn't go any further, I plopped my hands onto my knees and bent over, sucking in deep lungfuls of air. I was only wearing a sandwich shop t-shirt and a pair of high-waisted cotton shorts with my Converse, so I wasn't exactly dressed for exercise.

"Damn...you...wolf..." I wheezed.

He licked the back of my knee.

I let out a truly hideous screech, kicking and flailing at him. He easily sidestepped my half-hearted attempts to wound him, so I turned to threats instead. "Don't lick me if you want to survive."

I paused, gulping down air.

When I could breathe, I added, "I am not one of those people who touches every dog they see. Your germs are not welcome on this body." I gestured to all of me.

He gave a pathetic whine.

"I don't care what you think I am to you, werewolf. I know you were Veggie Guy, and I am not amused by any of this. I'm going home." I wiggled my finger at him like a crazy person. "So just sit there while I catch my breath, or go back to wherever the hell you and the rest of your not-football-team came from."

The wolf snorted, but he sat.

I bent back over, hands on my knees once again. I was still traveling alongside the dirt road, and though it felt like I'd been running forever, I would've walked for an entire week if it meant getting away from the werewolves and back to my dorm.

But it wasn't going to take an entire week. The paved road couldn't have been much further.

"Alright, Tea. You've got this. Just a little further, and you're home free," I lied to myself as I started jogging down the road again. The wolf made a weird sound, and I glanced at him. "What are you laughing at?"

He didn't answer, obviously.

Because he was a wolf.

Although, cartoon-style talking animals wouldn't be that crazy compared to what I'd just discovered existed.

"You are truly infuriating," I told him, shaking my head as I kept running. "I'm not going to be what you want. Your mate or whatever. That's not me. I've got dreams, and goals, and plans. I'm not going to be the housewife who sits at home and pops out a baby every year. I have school, and I have stuff to do, and things to accomplish. So just walk away. Go home." My voice raised as my rant continued.

The wolf ignored my lecture, his gaze on the forest in front of me.

I huffed, but kept running. It wasn't like I had another option. The kidnappers and their van were way behind me, and probably heading the opposite direction. After all, I was going back to my college town, and they'd been driving down the dirt road toward wherever they'd planned to take me.

Though it was suspicious that they hadn't come after me.

Were they just going to leave me with the wolf?

According to them, he was hunting me. And that was terrifying.

But shouldn't hunting be more violent than just running with me and refusing to leave?

I didn't know. And without the rest of the kidnappers, I had no one to ask.

Glancing at the wolf, it occurred to me that he hadn't had anything to do with the abduction. I mean, he'd been there, but he wasn't one of the guys who grabbed me. Jesse had started going wolf after meeting me, and the other guys grabbed us both.

He had clearly been with them, though. So he wasn't innocent, and I couldn't trust him.

Especially while he was furry.

A furry *werewolf*.

Dammit, that was a lot to wrap my head around.

I wheezed at him as we jogged (well, as I jogged and he trotted), "You should definitely choose someone else to be your mate. You and your kidnapper buddies are not my kind of guys, and I'm far from the easy, party-loving, sorority girl that guys like you are into."

My honey-blonde ponytail swayed behind me, reminding me why people sometimes assumed I was something other than the book-smart nerd I really was.

The wolf ignored me again.

Tired of being ignored, I shut my mouth and just kept on running. I was slow, but still moving.

It felt like an eternity later when I heard a car's engine behind me.

Cursing, I practically threw myself into a bush off to the side of the dirt road. Branches cut me and scratched me, but if it was Jesse's friends, I couldn't afford to get caught.

Jesse—or the wolf that had once been Jesse—crouched beside me, his body hidden by the bush even though he wasn't inside the damn thing like I was.

Sure enough, the kidnapper van passed us. They didn't even slow down.

When they were gone, the forest seemed even darker than it had before.

"I'm going to die out here," I mumbled to myself, as I slowly extricated my body from the bush. The wolf was licking me again, running his tongue over my cuts and scrapes. "Stop it, dammit. I don't know you." I shoved at his face.

He growled.

"Go find your wolfy friends and leave me to escape on my own." I tried to shoo him away. He barely budged. "Damn you." I sighed, then started walking down the dirt road.

I walked, and walked, and walked. By the time the sun was rising, I was *still* walking.

When I finally saw a flicker of light ahead of me, I let out a whoop of excitement and picked up my pace.

Abduction averted.

It wasn't until I reached the edge of town that I realized I'd celebrated too soon.

FOUR

THE BUILDINGS WERE A COMPLETELY different style than the new, modern builds of the college town I lived in.

I passed by a wind chime with at least fifty shells and bits of sea glass hanging from it. It looked homemade, which was odd considering we were surrounded by the forest and mountains, and nowhere near the beach. The wind chime hung over the porch of an old building covered in what looked like newly-painted, sky-blue siding. The building was small and old, but charming and looked well-taken-care-of.

Stopping out in front of the porch, I looked at the wolf beside me.

"You knew I wasn't walking back toward my school," I said, my voice flat.

He batted his eyes at me. I think he was trying to look innocent, but he was a *wolf*. He could definitely see better in the dark than I could.

Which meant that he'd played me.

The damn wolf had played me.

Abduction not averted.

I looked back at the door, weighing my options.

I could knock and hope there was someone sympathetic inside, who could give me some water, and maybe some bandages to wrap my poor, sad feet in. Maybe they'd give me a ride back to my dorm, too.

Or... maybe the wolf would kill them.

Yeah, not worth the risk to those poor, probably-nice people.

I resolved to keep walking until I found a police station. Or maybe an animal shelter. One or another of those places would have a way to get rid of my wolfy stalker.

And hopefully, a ride home.

I kept walking. My shoes were soaked on the inside, and I hoped they'd been soaked by pus from broken blisters, or maybe sweat. The alternative was blood, and that idea made me want to puke. The shoes were at least six years old, but the worn-down soles and holes in them hadn't done a thing to help prevent blisters while I was walking.

My phone was back in my locker at the sandwich shop, so I had no idea exactly what time it was, but it had to be pretty early in the morning. Yet, the town was surprisingly active.

That was also completely opposite of my college town. The university and its students didn't seem to fully wake up until noon, even though there were early classes offered too.

The further I walked into the city, the more I found it strange that no one commented on the wolf following me.

Seriously, who wouldn't be afraid of a wolf walking freely around town?

I guessed maybe he could pass for a dog, but he wasn't on a leash or anything.

We stopped at a gas station so I could ask directions, and I walked up to a woman filling up her car with gas. I selected her thinking she looked like she wasn't a murderer, and looked nice enough that she wouldn't be pissed by me distracting her from her task and asking where the police station was.

I forced a smile. "Hi, do you have a second?"

"Of course." She smiled back, glancing at Jesse. Like the others we'd passed, she didn't look alarmed to see him.

"Do you happen to know where the police station is?"

"Oh, you mean the main alpha's house? Sure, if you keep going down this street, you'll run into a logged mansion. The main alpha lives there, along with his pack."

Main alpha? What the hell?

"Are you a werewolf?" I asked bluntly.

It seemed like the only logical answer, given her weird acceptance of the wolf beside me and her strange answers to my questions. And yeah, there was no tact behind my words, but I was exhausted and in pain and confused.

She laughed. "Of course. Everyone in this town is a werewolf. Welcome to Moon Ridge, honey." She gave a big smile, and I took a step back. When I stepped back, I bumped into Jesse, who licked my leg *again*.

"I've lost my freaking mind," I mumbled, hurrying back down the road the way I'd come. The woman filling her gas tank yelled something after me, but my brain was too fried to listen.

It had taken me all night to walk to the werewolf town, but maybe I could get back to my dorm by the time the sun set. If I just kept walking, ignored my dry mouth and aching feet, I could make it.

What was the alternative; getting eaten by a damn werewolf or turning into one?

I'd take some foot pain and hunger over that any day.

The wolf realized my intentions and stepped between me and the forest before I got back on the dirt road. He gave a low, threatening growl.

"Get out of my way," I threatened back. My body swayed a bit, and I flung my arms out to try to keep my balance. I managed to remain standing, luckily.

Taking a step to the side, I tried to pass the wolf. He just jumped in my way again.

"Dammit, wolf, *move!*" I yelled.

Laughter erupted behind me.

I spun around, having no idea what to do with my hands if I was going to have to try to fight my way to freedom. Was I supposed to fist them? Or pull them up close to my chest, maybe?

There they were: the not-football-team. Of course those assholes were the source of the laughter.

That was just my freakin' luck.

In the light of day, it was easier to separate the not-football-players from each other. Five men of various ethnicities, sizes, clothing styles, and hair-cuts. Separate from each other in every way I could see, but with one thing in common:

They were all werewolves.

"I wish I could order my wolf around like that." Seatbelt Guy grinned. Now that I wasn't panicking, I got a better look at him. His skin was dark, his hair cut close to his scalp on the sides of his face and head. Slim, artfully-styled locs fell to the middle of his forehead. He was the tallest of the group, but only by an inch or so. They were all tall, and all built like the damn football players I'd assumed they were.

"We all do," another guy agreed. He strode toward me, offering a hand. He was tan, with a mass amount of fluffy, dark brown hair and a smile that would've set most people at ease.

But it just made me more wary.

I didn't take his hand.

"You assholes kidnap me, leave me with a monster, and want me to shake your hands and trust you? Yeah, right." I glared at the lot of them. "Take me home."

"Sorry, we can't do that." Smiley Guy pulled his hand away and gestured to the wolf behind me. "You've got a better chance at surviving the mating bite if you spend the weeks leading up to it with Jesse, at his place. We'll keep you fed and safe, but being alive is more important than being home."

I laughed, and the sound came out sounding slightly maniacal. I needed sleep, and painkillers, and freedom. "Bullshit. All of this is bullshit."

Jesse stepped up next to me and growled fiercely at the guys. Their expressions faltered a bit.

He lowered his nose to my shoe, a wolf's way of gesturing, I guess.

"Is your foot injured?" one of the guys asked. I was pretty sure he had been the getaway driver, though that didn't help much because I didn't know any of their names.

"No," I lied, not wanting them to have an excuse to grab me again.

Jesse growled again, and it sounded like he was disagreeing with me.

Damn wolf.

"Grab her. Let's get her back to Jesse's place so she's got some time to rest," Smiley Guy instructed.

"No, don't—"

Seatbelt Guy tossed me over his shoulder once again.

I kicked and yelled as the guys walked back to Main Street, then turned down another street, and then another. They chatted amongst themselves and Jesse trotted behind me as they went, as if they weren't dragging me along like a freakin' prisoner.

Eventually my throat got too dry for yelling, and my body too tired for kicking. And then I just gave up. I was carried along, draped over Seatbelt Guy's shoulder like a sack of potatoes and wondering what the hell I'd done so wrong to deserve being attacked and kidnapped by werewolves.

No one else in the town seemed to have a problem with my shouting for help—or seemed to see it as a problem. I'd determined that werewolf towns were full of sick monsters who were completely okay with abducting innocent people… and probably murdering them, too.

The not-football-team stopped in front of a row of townhouses and set me down, keeping a hand on my arm. In another situation, I would've thought the townhouses looked nice, maybe even cute. They were little two-story townhomes covered in siding, all of them painted differently with different accent colors and such, but all in the same shades of dove gray, dark green, and soft white.

They walked as a group to the house at the end of the row. It was mainly gray, with white as a secondary color and only hints of green. I liked the color combination the most on that one, not that I'd admit it out loud.

One of the guys typed the code into the garage door's keypad, and everyone headed into the house together. I eyed Jesse the wolf, who had started wagging his tail as we approached his space.

Wagging his freaking tail, after abducting me.

That wolf dude needed serious help.

Seatbelt Guy tossed me onto a dark blue loveseat, and said, "Welcome home, Teagan."

FIVE

I SAT up and shot him the most heated glare I could manage. "This is *not* my home. And I don't remember telling any of you monsters my name."

"It was on your shirt." Smiley Guy tapped his collarbone. "Your name tag fell off on the way to the van."

"You mean it fell off when you were *dragging me* to the van."

"Carrying you, actually," another of the guys corrected.

There were too many of the werewolves to keep them all straight.

I was so freakin' screwed.

"Well, if it bothers you that we know your name, I'm Elliot." Smiley Guy offered his hand.

"I'm Ford," Seatbelt Guy added.

The rest of them told me their names too, but they all went right over my head.

Jesse jumped up next to me on the couch. He dropped his big furry head to rest on my thigh, so I slid away from him. He scooted toward me in response, and I moved more.

That continued until my side met the arm rest, and then I was stuck… with a damn werewolf head on my bare thigh.

I should've worn leggings to work.

"We'll leave you two alone for now. Dinner's at Ford's place tonight, it's the one next door." Elliot, AKA Smiley, gestured off to the side. "Get some rest, and a shower. You reek. We'll find you some clothes, but for now, just wear Jesse's."

"You guys are insane." I scowled at them. "This is crazy."

"Yup. Welcome to Moon Ridge." Elliot grinned.

He was the second person to say that, yet somehow after hearing it twice, I felt even less welcome.

They all left, and I watched until the door closed behind them.

And… they had to be completely out of their minds if they thought I was going to stay in Jesse's house.

I slid off the couch, hurrying toward the door. It was true that I stank; I was a sweaty mess, and my feet were either soaked with sweat, pus-covered, or bloody, and hurting something awful. But my life was my priority.

I found a key-hook by the door, and a perfectly good set of keys hanging off it.

Bingo.

I sprinted back to the garage door I'd just been carried inside through.

A scream tore through my throat when the wolf smoothly jumped over the couch, landing between me and the door a fraction of a second before I reached it.

"What the hell?" I screeched. "Get out of my way!"

The wolf growled. Somehow, I could tell it wasn't a threatening growl...more like an answer. A simple, "No."

I raced toward the front door.

He had no problem beating me there, too.

"Damn you." My hands clenched in fists around the keys. I released the fists, shoved the keys into my pocket, and headed for the stairs.

I'd have to take a shower, then make my escape while Jesse was napping. Wolves slept as much as dogs, right?

The wolf jumped up a couple steps, then walked up the stairs with me at my pace. Every step was excruciating given the mess that was my feet, but I pushed through.

At the top of the stairs, there were two bedrooms and one bathroom. I ducked inside the first bedroom and determined it was Jesse's. His closet was a smallish walk-in, but a couple of the racks were empty like he was expecting someone else to move their stuff in too.

I grabbed one of his shirts from the closet and opened the drawers, rifling around until I found a pair of his sweats. It was still too hot outside for sweats, given that we lived in Northern Georgia and it was September, but what looked like his shorts' drawer was empty. And I wasn't going to wear the man's boxer-briefs; I didn't even know him.

Glancing down at my feet, I thought about the suspicious wetness in my shoes and reached into another of Jesse's drawers, grabbing some of his socks, too.

I needed to cover those suckers so they didn't leak blood and/or pus everywhere. I didn't care about my kidnapper's house staying clean, but if I couldn't escape, I wasn't about to walk all over my own dried foot pus.

After shutting the drawers and then closing the closet door too, I headed into the bathroom. The wolf followed me in before I could shut the door to keep him out.

"Out." I commanded, pointing to the door.

He plopped down on the bath mat. The shower's curtain was dark blue and only a little see-through, but I still didn't want to shower in there, all exposed to the wolf.

"Seriously, get out," I snapped.

Jesse wasn't just a wolf—he was a man too. That was easy to forget, but not when I was getting in the damn shower.

I looked around for a weapon. Like a broom, or maybe a razor...

All I found was a bottle of Febreze spray, and one of those electric face shavers with three disc-looking things to trim facial hair.

I grabbed the Febreze and pointed it at the werewolf.

"Get out or you'll be eating perfume," I snarled. Really, the sound could've rivaled the one the wolf had made earlier. "I'm exhausted and in pain, this is not the time to mess with me."

The wolf sat up straight at that, and gave a soft growl.

"Don't you growl at me for threatening you. You're the asshole who kidnapped me and trapped me in your house, wolf."

He leaned his nose to my foot and sniffed, then growled louder.

What the hell was wrong with him?

He nudged at my shoes with his nose. When I didn't do anything in response but glare down at him, he carefully caught one of my shoelaces between his teeth and gave a gentle tug until the lace came undone.

"You want me to take my shoes off?" I asked, incredulously.

The wolf looked at me and bobbed his head vigorously.

"You're out of your damn mind," I muttered, but sat on the closed toilet-seat anyway. I eased my shoe off my foot carefully, wincing and cursing a couple times as it came off. My sock was soaked, and the white fabric was stained red in a couple places. In other places, it was the yellowish color of pus.

Blood *and* pus. Yay.

My eyes started to sting as I peeled my sock off my foot, and I bit down hard on the inside of my cheek to stop from crying out.

Jesse started whining, trying to put his nose up close to my injury. I swatted him away, but he remained close and kept whining.

I did the same with my other shoe and sock, and had the same results.

Intense pain.

Massive blisters on my heels, toes, and the backs of my ankles.

Apparently I should've worn athletic shoes *and* leggings to work.

"Happy?" I grumbled at the wolf, who was still whining. "Me neither." I leaned my back against the toilet, my eyes closing as my body relaxed just a little. "Damn, I'm tired."

Jesse poked my leg gently with his nose, then poked the cupboard beneath the bathroom sink. With a dramatic sigh,

I leaned over and pulled it open for him. He dug around for a minute before dragging out a small red fabric bag with a white cross on it.

"A first-aid kit? That's actually helpful, thanks." I took it from him.

He sat down and watched me pull some things out.

"I don't know much about first aid. I've never really been injured before," I rambled as I spread items out on the ground in front of me to take stock of what I had. "Other than the usual scraped knees and neck-burns from curling-iron fails, of course. But I've never broken a bone or had anything like this before." I gestured to my feet.

He made a weird noise.

"I have no idea what that's supposed to mean," I told him. "I don't speak wolf."

The noise of frustration that followed, I did understand.

He gestured toward my foot with his nose, then went up on his back legs and stuck his nose in the sink.

"You want me to put my foot in the sink?" I checked.

He bobbed his head, then gestured to a bottle of hand soap beside the sink.

"You want me to wash my horribly raw feet with *hand soap*?" My eyebrows shot into my forehead.

He nodded again.

I had no idea what else to do. With a sigh/groan, I forced myself back to my feet and carefully lifted one of the raw devils into the sink. I had to contort my leg to do it, and resting my weight on the other foot was hell, but I managed.

Lifting the handle on the faucet, I put it on warm and hissed when the water flowed over my burning, throbbing skin.

The wolf bumped the handle with his nose, setting the temperature right in-between cold and hot.

The water ran over my foot until the throbbing faded to a dull, aching pain. Jesse hit the soap bottle with his nose, and I sighed again.

But, since I didn't have any other ideas, I shut off the water and pumped a little soap into my hand. While I cleaned the area gently, I flooded the bathroom with enough curses to make a pirate grin.

After a minute, Jesse bumped my hand to stop me from scrubbing, then flipped the water back on. He took care to make sure it was right in the middle between hot and cold again.

More cursing ensued when I rinsed off the bubbles, and even more when Jesse shut off the water and gestured to my other foot.

I repeated the process with foot two, then finally sat back down on the lid of the toilet seat. And honestly, I'd never been so thrilled to sit on a toilet in my life.

Since my feet were still dripping wet, I reached for a towel. Jesse growled, and I jerked my hands away.

His growling stopped instantly.

Looking at him curiously, I reached my hand toward the towel again, just to see what he'd do.

Sure enough, he growled again the moment my fingers were nearing the towel.

"You want them to air-dry?" I checked.

He bobbed his head.

"Alright." I shrugged.

He wiggled beneath my legs, lifting them up so I was using his back as a leg-rest while my feet dried off.

He was warm and fuzzy, so it was actually kind of relaxing. The pain eased a bit with my weight off my feet, so I leaned my head back awkwardly against the toilet seat and shut my eyes.

I MANAGED to doze off until my leg-rest began to rumble with a growl.

Yawning, I sat up.

Damn, my body hurt.

"What now?" I asked the wolf.

He slowly slid out from under me, his eyes sweeping the medical supplies on the ground. His nose touched a tube I recognized, and I picked it up.

Triple Antibiotic Ointment.

Maybe he did know what he was doing.

He used his nose to gesture to the bottoms of my feet.

"I know how to use this," I told him.

It took me a while to spread it over my blisters. When that was done, the wolf pointed to some square-shaped gauze pads and a roll of what looked like tape.

I slapped the gauze on my feet, used a little tape to keep it there, and then grabbed Jesse's socks off the ground. Wrestling one on without too much pain or swearing, I looked over at the other sock and stared for a minute.

"Dammit," I finally said.

The wolf tilted his head. It was kind of adorable, not that I'd admit it.

"I haven't showered yet. I stink," I gestured to my feet. "I'm going to have to redo all of this."

The wolf shook his head at me. He gestured to the shower, which was one of those combination shower-tubs.

I waited for more of an explanation.

He hopped into the tub with ease, then rolled to his back. His back legs popped over the edge of the tub, and he wiggled them around.

"Clever bastard," I muttered, shaking my head as I eased the second sock on. "Now, out." I pointed to the door.

He gave me puppy dog eyes, and I grabbed the Febreze again. "I will use this."

SIX

THE WOLF HEAVED a sigh but then moved toward the door. His eyes swept the room as he went; he was looking for an escape route just to make sure I couldn't leave, probably.

I'd already looked though, and there wasn't one.

Satisfied that I was good and trapped, he stepped into the hallway and plopped down on his belly right in front of the door.

With the comfort of the door separating us, I took my time in the bathtub. Mostly because I wanted some distance from the wolf.

Er, Jesse.

He'd started to seem too human when he was giving me directions via our little game of Charades. And I didn't want to humanize him. He and his friends had abducted me, and they were trapping me in the townhouse.

I was not going to fall victim to Stockholm Syndrome. And sure, I was a long way from that, but the first step to falling for your kidnapper was seeing them as a person with hopes and dreams and feelings and shit.

At least, I assumed that was the first step. Taking Psych 101 during my spring semester had led to me feeling like I understood people better than I really did though.

Anyway, bathing in his bathtub was weird. Washing with Jesse's shower gel was weirder. Shaving my armpits and legs with the man's face-razor seemed like a sin, so I left them hairy.

I did wonder why he needed a razor in the shower when the electric one was sitting on the counter, but since he wasn't available for asking, I let it go.

As I rinsed shampoo from my hair, I tried to think back to the night before. None of the men had really stood out to me then, since I was so focused on trying to get out of the sandwich shop without catching the attention of one of the beefy guys. I couldn't even recall what Jesse looked like.

But he had conditioner sitting next to his shampoo, so I knew he wasn't bald.

I sniffed the conditioner. It matched the generic bottle of shampoo I'd used. I liked the scent but couldn't put my finger on what it actually smelled like. The name was *River*

Rocks, and I didn't know what a *river rock* smelled like, but I was 99% sure it wasn't the same as the smell of the product in that bottle.

Why did men's shower products never smell like real things the way women's smelled like fruit and flowers?

My favorite scent was Sparkling Champagne. Though I'd never actually tasted champagne, every time I smelled the shower gel, lotion, and perfume, I about died and went to heaven. There was something so satisfying about using shower products that smelled amazing.

After I got out and dried off, I got dressed. And as weird as I felt washing in Jesse's tub, using all of his soaps and things, I felt so much weirder putting his pants on. My bra and underwear were absolutely disgusting, so I couldn't put even those back on without a good, heavy wash.

So, I was free-boobing and free-buffing. None of my parts were loving the extra airflow as I shuffled out of the bathroom with an arm around my chest, my clothes bundled in my other arm. My lack of exercise had made me soft in the chest, thighs, butt, and arms, and my curves did *not* know how to feel about their sudden freedom.

Jesse trotted beside me as I gingerly made my way back downstairs, heading to the clothing washer and dryer I'd seen tucked in a corner near the garage door. My feet were hurting something fierce. Painkillers were going to be my next focus after I got my underwear going in the wash.

When the machine was spinning, I looked at Jesse. The wolf peered back, his tail wagging once again.

"Where do you keep your painkillers?" I asked him.

He led me into the kitchen, and went up on his hind legs to point straight up at the cabinet beside the fridge. I opened it and breathed a sigh of relief when I found Tylenol, Ibuprofen, and Excedrin too. Oddly enough, every one of the bottles was still sealed shut, like they'd only recently been purchased.

After I thanked the wolf, I opened cupboards until I found a glass for water, then filled it up in the sink before swallowing the proper dose of both Ibuprofen and Tylenol.

I set the cup down beside the sink and headed for the fridge. Pulling it open, my eyebrows lifted at the assload of food in front of me.

At least two dozen containers of yogurt were stacked along the side of the top shelf, five packages of bagels cuddled up against them. Four 18-egg cartons rested against the bagels, maxing out the shelf's space. The shelf below it was similarly packed in with lunch foods instead of breakfast, and the one below that looked like dinner leftovers and ingredients.

Even the door was loaded with a gallon of milk, a gallon of chocolate milk, a bunch of premade smoothies, and every condiment in existence.

"How many people live here?" I looked at the wolf.

He tilted his head, confused again.

I gestured to the fully-packed fridge. "There's enough food here to feed five or six people for a week."

Understanding dawned in his eyes. He lifted a paw and circled it around, then gestured back to his chest.

"You're the only one who lives here?" I checked my understanding of round two in our wolfy game of charades.

He bobbed his head.

"You eat this much food?" I gestured to the fridge again.

He bobbed again.

"Damn. Werewolves must have massive grocery bills." I turned back to the fridge. Down on the dinner shelf, I saw what looked like leftover pizza and grabbed it.

After I heated it up, I demolished three pieces without even pausing to sit down at the table and get off my throbbing feet, and then groaned.

So full.

The wolf growled at me.

"What are you grumping about now?" I shot him a tired stare.

He went up on his back legs, leaned over the table, and caught the bag of pizza between his teeth. Dragging it over to me, he set it on my plate and nodded toward it.

"You want me to eat more?" My eyebrows lifted.

He nodded again.

"I'm stuffed. I'll puke if I eat anything else."

He looked concerned.

When had I decided he could look concerned?

When had I decided he had real, human emotions at all?

Dammit, I was already going all Stockholmy.

A massive yawn stopped my thoughts in their tracks.

The only bed in the house belonged to Jesse, and I was not sleeping in my kidnapper's bed, regardless of what form he was in.

I looked around the kitchen again, and my eyes caught on the calendar. It had been Tuesday night when I was abducted, which meant I'd already missed my Wednesday classes. It would be hard to make up for missing one day considering I was enrolled in a shitload of classes, but I could handle it. If I missed Friday too, that would be much more difficult.

But I was escaping in the very near future, so I told myself it wouldn't be a problem.

I tossed the rest of the pizza leftovers back in the fridge and shuffled to the living room. The couch in there had been comfortable, so it would be fine for a nap. I would wake up while Jesse was still asleep, and then I'd take his car and get the hell out of Moon Ridge before any more shit happened.

I sprawled out on the generous-sized couch, lying on my side and curling my stomach up against the back cushions. The couch smelled good—really good.

I didn't want to consider who had sat on it to make it smell so good.

Shutting my eyes, I waited for sleep to take me. Just as I started to fall asleep, there was a dip in the couch near my feet. A warm weight brushed against the bottoms of them, and I winced at the pain that ensued.

The weight disappeared instantly, and a soft whine left the wolf as he moved.

I started to drift off again, and then the couch dipped at my back. Furry heat rested against me, and it felt heavenly.

But I was going to resist Stockholm Syndrome if it killed me.

"Get off." My first command was firm, but not cruel.

The wolf whined and didn't move.

I turned my head, looking at him over my shoulder. Our eyes collided, and I shuddered.

Those bright red orbs were freaky as hell, especially up close.

The wolf whined again.

"Get off the couch. I didn't invite you to cuddle, and I know you're as much of a guy as you are an animal. We are *not* sleeping together."

He stood on reluctant legs and slipped off the couch, lowering to his belly on the ground. Though he rested right against the base of the couch, he wasn't touching me, and that was good enough.

I got comfortable again and shut my eyes, falling asleep almost instantly.

I SLEPT PEACEFULLY for a good long while until a male voice tugged me back to reality.

"Damn, that girl could sleep through a hurricane."

A growl right next to me shook me awake.

I sat up suddenly, jerking my head around the room to see what was going on.

"Sorry, bud. Didn't mean to wake her up." Ford's hands were lifted beside his head in surrender.

He was talking to the wolf.

At least I wasn't the only one who did that.

I looked around the room again, eyes bleary as I tried to remember where I was and what was going on.

Kidnapped, trapped by a wolf, leftover pizza... right.

"I brought you some clothes, courtesy of Jesse's mom. She's excited to meet you, after you're a wolf too of course."

Of course?

Wait, his mom?

What the hell?

"What is this, an arranged marriage?" I blurted.

Ford shrugged. "Kind of. You'll figure it out."

"No, I won't *figure it out*. I have a full-ride scholarship to one of the best schools in the country. I can't afford to miss the time I've already missed thanks to this...whatever this is." I flung my hand out toward the wolf still lying vigilantly on the ground beside my couch. "I need to get back to my dorm, back to the campus, back to my classes."

"Then ask the wolf to bite you."

SEVEN

"YOU ARE COMPLETELY INSANE," I looked around for something to throw at him but came up empty-handed.

"The wolves are dicks, but they do understand the human world. If he bites you, you'll become one of us. Or die, but that's not likely."

"You're talking about them like they're separate from you."

I'd deal with the death thing afterward.

"They are separate from us."

My eyebrows lifted.

"I know it sounds crazy." Ford jumped up on the counter, his gigantic legs dangling off the edge.

Damn, he was gorgeous.

Jesse growled at him, and he slid back to his feet.

"Basically, a werewolf is like this." He grabbed the salt and pepper shakers off the counter and held them toward me. "This is the human." He shook the salt around. "This is the wolf." He shook the pepper. "Two completely separate living beings. A long time ago, a wolf and a human became friends. They pissed off a witch coven—a really damn powerful one—and the witches combined their magic to trap the wolf and human in one body."

Ford plopped the saltshaker on top of the peppershaker. "They created the first werewolf, and assumed he wouldn't be able to reproduce, which added another level to the punishment. But nature has rules, and not even witches can go against those rules. His wolf found a human mate and hunted her, then when he bit her, she became like him. They popped out a couple babies, and the babies found human mates and popped out more babies, and so on." He dropped the saltshakers.

"You're two beings in one body; that doesn't make you two separate beings," I countered.

"Well, actually," he grabbed the salt and pepper again, stacking them on top of each other like he had before. "Imagine it like this. The wolf and the human share one form, but two entire bodies and souls and minds. There's no magic that makes it possible for us to communicate, so we're stuck. The wolves are stuck with humans, watching the world through the human's eyes without a way to interact with the person they're pretty much riding inside, and the humans are stuck with animals they have no way to control or communicate with."

Well, that did make more sense.

"Then why do you call the wolf Jesse?"

"That was the name his parents gave him." Ford shrugged. "We're trapped in one form; it makes sense to go by one name."

"So when you say the wolf is hunting me..."

"Jesse the *wolf* is hunting you. He'll have complete control of their body until he bites you," Ford confirmed. "But he wants you to *want* to be bitten, because history has proved that if you're okay with it, you've got a better chance at surviving."

"And what's going to happen when Jesse the man takes over for Jesse the wolf?" I checked.

Ford dropped the salt and pepper again and scratched the back of his neck.

Was he blushing?

"The mating call works on werewolves both in wolf and human form. For wolves, it's the hunting. For humans, it's lust."

"Lust?" My voice raised an octave.

Ford nodded.

I waited for more of an explanation, but it didn't come.

"You're telling me that after this wolf bites me, I'm going to have an ultra-horny guy trying to rape me?!" I demanded.

"No, no, no." Ford held his hands out in front of himself, telling me to stop. "The wolves inside us are focused on one thing: family. It's the center of our society, and why we work in packs. Me and the other guys you met, we're all Jesse's pack."

He explained, "There's this human idea about alphas being assholes who charm the pants off everything with a vagina and take what they want no matter what, but that's not how wolves are. In the wild, an alpha wolf is the dad of the pack. His mate and his kids make up the rest of the pack, and he protects them above all else. That's why Jesse the wolf was growling at us when you hit your head in the van; his first priority is protecting you, his mate. He could never rape you or anyone else, because he could never *hurt* you."

"He's going to bite me." I folded my arms. "I'd call that hurting me."

"That's not something he can control. Nature forces it on him. His hunt is basically his attempt to ready you for the bite... and werewolf venom numbs pain, so it doesn't actually hurt you. The numbing venom even makes your first shift painless, unlike every other one will be."

Yeah, *that* really made me want to be a werewolf.

"So Jesse the man has no way to communicate with his wolf right now?" I checked.

"Right."

"And the wolf is just a really intelligent animal."

"Yep." He popped the "p" with his mouth.

"Basically, like a dog," I added.

"Basically."

"This is a lot," I groaned.

I would still try to escape, but it was looking like the wolf might outlast me when it came to my escape attempts.

"If all of this is definite, and there's nothing I can do to stop it, why can't I just bring the wolf back to my place with me?" I asked.

Ford paused.

Ha.

Looked like I'd caught him.

"This is Jesse's territory. He's comfortable here, and for a wolf, comfort means patience. If you stay here with him, you'll buy yourself some more time before nature forces him to bite you. And the longer the hunt goes on, the longer you stay human," he explained.

Why couldn't they have told me all that shit before kidnapping me?

I mean, I probably wouldn't have listened. Even though I was now listening, I wasn't really taking every detail in at the moment.

But if they'd told me, it would've gone a long way toward making me less terrified.

"If that's the case, I don't see why I can't keep going to school. I could take Jesse with me, and come back here to do my homework afterward," I explained.

The conversation was starting to feel a bit too Stockholm Syndrome-ish.

The wolf growled.

Ford chuckled. "If you were working with a human, you probably could. But a wolf would have to believe you were actually going to come back, and that would take time."

"What if I take a human with me too?" I looked at Jesse. "Ford could come along in the car. Attendance isn't mandatory in a couple of my classes, but there are two that I can't miss if I want A's. And I don't want A's; I *need* A's."

The wolf growled.

That would be a no.

"She's just going to keep trying to escape if you don't let her go, buddy." Ford gestured to Jesse.

Jesse growled again, this time at Ford. And this time, much more menacingly.

Ford headed for the door. "Alright, I'll get out of your hair. Dinner's going to be ready in twenty minutes, so come over or we'll come get you," he called over his shoulder as he left.

The door shut behind him, and I turned to Jesse.

"I won't ever give you a chance if you cost me my scholarship," I told him, my voice low. "I have to be in class at 8 AM on Friday, and you can either take me or I can try to get there myself."

The wolf huffed.

I left him at the foot of the couch, carefully heading back to the kitchen to check out the clothes Ford had left in the kitchen for me.

Plain black leggings and a faded concert t-shirt waited with a simple thong and sports bra. It felt weird to accept underwear from the mom of the wolf who'd abducted me, but I had to wear *something*. And the bra and underwear had tags, reassuring me that the stuff hadn't been worn before.

I had a fairly eclectic style and wore some of everything when it came to underwear and clothes both, since I'd always shopped at thrift stores for everything but bras and panties. I would pretty much wear anything, so an old band t-shirt and leggings were great.

I walked slowly to the laundry machines and checked my clothes—clean, but still wet. After switching them to the dryer, I carried the new clothes to the bathroom.

Quickly, I tried to close the bathroom door behind me. Jesse snarled and shoved his way in, forcing through the door and brushing past my hip to make space for himself.

"Seriously?" I groaned, scrubbing my hand over my face. "Can you not fight me for just one minute?"

He gestured with his nose and I looked at what he was pointing to.

The window.

A skinny blip of a thing, above the shower/tub combo.

"Really? My thigh couldn't even fit through that window, let alone this monstrosity I call a head," I pointed to my head, which I admittedly found too large for my body. Though, I'd heard from other girls that they felt the same way, and from others that they felt the opposite too, so I only felt slightly crazy because of it.

He growled at me, standing up on his back paws. His front paws met my shoulders, and he licked up my face.

"You have *got* to stop doing that," I grumbled. "I get it; you like me. But you kidnapped me, so the liking is *not* mutual."

He whined.

"Oh, shush." I pushed him toward the door. "Regardless of whether my head is oversized or normal sized, it's not fitting through that window. So scram."

EIGHT

HE MUST'VE BELIEVED ME, because he finally left, and getting dressed after he was gone was quick even with my injured feet.

No way in hell was I putting shoes back on, so I just headed out with my socked feet. Every footstep hurt more than the last, but I braved my way to the front porch with Jesse at my side. The porch had a comfortable-looking hammock swinging across it, and I itched to sit in it and just swing for a bit but reminded myself that I'd been kidnapped.

And there was no Stockholm Syndrome allowed.

Jesse growled before I stepped off the porch.

"I'm getting really tired of getting growled at. And licked. And pretty much everything else that has to do with you being a *wolf*." I narrowed my eyes at him. "We aren't friends, okay? You think I'm your mate, but you kidnapped me. I don't like you."

He scowled.

Turning, he trotted toward the house next door.

I went to step off the stairs, but like he had eyes on the back of his head, he gave a warning growl.

"Damn wolf," I muttered.

I was saying that a lot, wasn't I?

What was he even doing?

I didn't know, but I stayed on the porch, giving him a minute for whatever he had planned.

He came back thirty seconds later, with Smiley in tow.

What was Smiley's name again?

Eli?

Dammit, I needed to pay more attention.

"Looks like you need a little help," Smiley called out as he approached.

"If you're offering to help, I'll take a ride home. I'll even agree not to go tell the police about the kidnapping werewolves of Moon Ridge if you take me back right now."

He grinned. "The cops already know about us. Why else haven't you heard about all the other abductions from your college over the past few decades?"

My eyes widened.

Seriously?

He scooped me up off the ground without asking permission. I fought his grip, attempting to get free, but the man was just as buff and football-player-esque as the rest of the guys.

I expected him to set me down when we reached the house, but instead, he hauled me all the way to Ford's kitchen table before setting me down in one of the chairs.

"Wolves are protective," he explained to me as he stepped back. "Jesse doesn't like you walking around if it hurts your feet."

"I noticed," I drawled. Looking around the kitchen, which was loaded with all five of the pack's men, plus Jesse, I wondered aloud, "Where are the rest of your mates?"

One of the guys smirked. I didn't recognize him, even though I was sure he'd been with the group earlier. He had long brown hair tied up in a man-bun on the top but shaved on the sides, his face made up of sharp angles and well-trimmed stubble barely long enough to consider it a beard. "Not a clue. Our wolves don't warn us before they choose a mate, though they do start nesting."

"Nesting? Like a pregnant woman?" I asked incredulously.

"Yup. They make us buy extra crap, clean out our freezers, get our houses nice and tidy. Shit like that," he explained.

"I should probably already know, but what's your name again?" I asked. I assumed the question would offend him, but didn't really care. I needed to know all of their names in case they were lying about the cops being in on this werewolf shit.

"I'm Zed. We grow up being trained for this, warned that joining a pack is a lot for a human who's used to being on their own for the most part. Forgetting a name isn't a big deal."

Wow. That was surprisingly courteous...and surprisingly creepy, too.

"Your parents prepare you for kidnapping humans?" I asked incredulously.

"How else are we supposed to get our mates into our houses right after we meet them, while trapped in our wolf forms?"

Okay, that was almost a valid question.

Almost.

Minus the abducting-innocent-humans part.

"You could have one of your other pack-friends try to woo the human girls into coming here before you sic a wolf on them," I suggested.

Another of the guys whose names I didn't remember dropped into the chair beside Zed. He was almost as pale as I was, with scruffy blonde hair and an equally scruffy beard. "Ha!" He snorted and looked at Jesse. "You picked a funny one."

I scowled. "Why is that funny?"

"One of us flirting with another wolf's mate would pretty much be like declaring war. There's not a wolf in the world who would accept another man hitting on his woman. Our wolves are protective first, and possessive second."

"Really?" I frowned.

I'd just determined that they *weren't* possessive though.

"He let Eli carry me here." I gestured to Jesse's house, and then to Smiley. I still couldn't remember the second half of his name, so I shortened it.

"Elliot," Smiley called out from the kitchen, also not offended by my forgetfulness.

"And pretty much all of you have touched me at one point or another, though not...sexily."

Sexily? Geeze, I was going to get myself in trouble if I kept making words up and guessing names.

The scruffy guy grinned. "*Not sexily* is the key part of that phrase. We're all packmates, which means we're brothers. Jesse trusts us, but not infinitely. If we hit on you, he'd still try to kill us."

So theoretically... I could get myself out of Moon Ridge by kissing his packmates so the wolf attacked them.

It wasn't the most ethical plan I'd ever had, but it could save my life from a bunch of werewolves, so I'd roll with it.

"What was your name again?" I asked Scruffy Guy.

"Rocco." He was still grinning.

And the perfect first target.

"Sexy name," I remarked.

Rocco's grin faltered.

Zed's eyes narrowed.

Perfect. I had the absolute perfect plan.

Minus the brothers killing each other, but I doubted that would actually happen if I was the one flirting and not them.

Jesse eyed me suspiciously, jumping up in the chair beside mine and sitting.

"So what are you studying, Teagan?" Smiley called out from the kitchen, smoothing over the tension my comment had created.

I liked the tension, though. Tension was going to save my ass.

My real major was nursing, but it wasn't the time for real majors.

"Public relations."

"Public...relations?" Zed lifted an eyebrow. Rocco lifted two.

"Yes sir." I smiled.

Honestly, I wasn't sure what classes a public relations major would even take, but I thought the name of the major might make their minds go to *sexual* relations.

Ford's suspicious gaze landed on me. "You're acting weird."

"Isn't this how you wanted me to act when you kidnapped me?" I drawled. "Agreeable?"

Jesse growled at me, and I ignored him. Instead of responding to his grumpiness, I changed the subject abruptly. "Where's your bathroom?"

If I was going to make things more tense and uncomfortable, I needed to be wearing less clothes.

"I'll show you," Rocco offered, coming around the table. As I hoped, he picked me up out of the chair and carried me toward the bathroom.

The wolf didn't even realize that his protectiveness was going to work against him. And damn, I was enjoying feeling evil.

Jesse trotted beside us, and I leaned my head against Rocco's chest. I was so far from comfortable doing it that it wasn't even funny, but comfort would be sacrificed in favor of survival every time around.

I tugged my hair out of its ponytail, letting it fall against Rocco's arm as he walked. I hadn't brushed it out, but I knew guys liked the just-woke-up look sometimes.

"Thanks for the ride," I gave Rocco what I hoped was a sly smile and kissed his cheek before he set me down.

The wolf growled at his friend/brother, and I bit back a grin as I shut the door behind me.

Evil. So, so evil.

I analyzed myself in the mirror. I didn't own many sexy outfits because I didn't particularly like the attention they attracted, but I knew how to make my curves work for me.

First things first: the shirt had to go. With the faded concert t-shirt on, I looked cute. Without it, I had on leggings and a sports bra... AKA workout clothes, and what guy didn't like workout clothes on a girl?

I pulled up my boobs a bit, making my cleavage spill a bit out the top of the already-tight sports bra. Next, I finger-brushed my hair to get rid of some of the tangles, tugging the blonde locks over my shoulders so they framed my curves.

Stepping over to the toilet, I flushed it just so the guys wouldn't be suspicious. Then I washed my hands, because who knew what germs were on Ford's toilet.

The house looked clean and modern, but men were gross.

I opened the door and walked right up to Rocco, wrapping my arms around his neck. "I'm ready for a ride." I had to bite back a laugh at myself, because I knew the guys would take the comment sexually.

Jesse's snarl told me he had, and Rocco's red face said the same.

"Right. Okay." Rocco lifted me up off my feet, carrying me honeymoon-style toward the kitchen. His eyes were focused away from my exposed stomach and cleavage. "Do you want me to turn the AC on? We could cool it down in here if you're feeling warm."

I laughed.

Bold Teagan, coming right up.

"Oh, no. I just prefer not to wear shirts when it's avoidable. I figured I'd come over and check out the crowd, see if it would make anyone uncomfortable first before stripping. But you all are just so welcoming, I realized I was being silly to hide who I really am." I wrapped my fingers around his bicep. "Wow, you're so strong."

Rocco's expression was bordering on panic at that point, so I was positively gleeful.

I lifted my fingers to his face, brushing my hand over his scruffy beard.

Damn, I was good.

Or terrible, depending on your perspective, but I was going with good.

Rocco grabbed my wrist, tugging it away from his face as he stepped back into the kitchen. "I'm not really—"

I grabbed him around the neck, pressing my lips to his.

Go big or go home, right?

I'd had a couple of boyfriends, though none of them had been serious. But if there was one thing I'd learned, it was that little kisses on the lips didn't feel intimate to me. So kissing Rocco? Easy. No conscience required.

Rocco dropped me into a chair just as Jesse the wolf lunged for his throat.

I bit back a grin as I leaned away, only to get confronted by another of the guys.

Elliot began, "Teagan, what—"

I cut him off with a kiss to his mouth, too.

The more the merrier.

Jesse roared, and Elliot stepped away from me just in time to get tackled by the wolf.

One last guy would ensure proper, full-out chaos, so I grabbed Ford by the shirt and smacked my lips to his. He shook his head at me, but the respect in his eyes told me he knew exactly what I was doing.

And, just like Elliot had, he ducked away from me just before he was tackled.

The other guys were trying to calm the wolf as well as keep him from ripping into the ones I'd kissed. One of them had started shifting too at one point—which wasn't a short process—and the house was loud and crazy.

Stepping to the side of the room, I grabbed Ford's keys off a hook on his garage door and silently slipped away from the chaos. When I got outside, I climbed into the sporty silver car without a moment of hesitation.

Hitting the buttons to start the engine and open the garage at the same time, I prepped myself for wolves to run out into the garage and try to stop me.

They didn't come.

When the garage door was far enough open, I reversed faster than I ever had in my whole damn life and then peeled away from the house.

Free at last.

NINE

I GLANCED over my shoulder and into the rearview mirror a thousand times on my way through the town. Luckily, Moon Ridge was small enough that I didn't have a problem finding the dirt road that would lead me back home. And luckily, my abductors didn't catch up to me.

I flew down that dirt road way too fast for comfort, but comfort went out the window the moment I was kidnapped.

And frankly, I wasn't sure I'd ever get that comfort back.

But my life was still mine, and I was going to live it to the best of my damn ability until the day that wolf found me and bit me.

As the dirt road ended, I remembered that I'd left my phone and keys in my locker at the sub shop. That would be a good place to ditch Ford's car, too, since they already knew

I worked there. But parking there would mean walking, and I was not only shoeless, but injured.

I let out a small groan, knowing I'd just have to deal with it.

After parking in the sandwich shop's lot, I hurried out of the car. There was no time to waste. Entering through the employee entrance, I thanked my lucky stars when the break room was empty.

Stepping up to my locker, my shaky fingers twisted the spinner to undo the combination lock. It took two tries, but when it was open, I grabbed my backpack out of the locker and hugged it to my chest.

Finally, something from my normal life.

Something safe.

I pulled my phone out and slid the backpack's straps over my arms, far too aware that I was only wearing a bra, leggings, and socks.

"Tea," my manager called from behind me.

Dammit.

With a silent groan, I turned to face him.

"Hi, Warren." I forced a smile.

"You're not supposed to work until tonight. You missed me, didn't you?" he teased.

"Yep, that's it." I laughed nervously, tucking my hair behind my ear.

"Look, I'm sorry for the last-minute notice, but I can't work tonight." I paused. "Or ever again. I'm going to have to quit. I'm sorry." I tried not to cringe at my overuse of the word "sorry," but sometimes words just came out of my mouth without me realizing I was saying them or thinking them at all.

"What?" Warren's eyebrows shot upward. "You're our best employee."

"I know, but something happened, and I just—I have to quit. And I'm sorry, but I have to go right now. Bye."

I practically ran out of there.

If not for my feet, I would've been running for sure.

"Wait, Teagan!" Warren called after me. "Can't we at least talk about it?"

I waved a hand in the air over my shoulder to say no, hurrying down the sidewalk.

Every step burned, but I forced myself to keep moving.

I was not going to be caught by Jesse or any of the other Moon Ridge wolves again. I wasn't going to be a damn werewolf-mate, or a mail-order bride they kidnapped instead of paying.

As I went, my gaze caught on a bus stop. I never rode the bus, since pretty much everywhere I needed to go was within walking distance. My roommate had a car, and she'd drive me on the rare occasion I needed to go further than I could walk.

Glancing down at my feet, I remembered that wolves were hunters and that they were good at sniffing things out. If Jesse was hunting me, my wounded, socked feet were probably leaving an easy trail.

And… I wasn't going to be an easy catch.

At least, not a second time.

I slipped off the socks and then tucked them under a bush off the sidewalk. Littering wasn't something I'd normally do, but for the sake of fooling a couple of dangerous animals, I figured Mother Nature would understand.

Hobbling across the road, I ducked to the side of the bus stop so the metal canopy structure would block me from the sight of the sandwich shop. When the werewolves came looking, I didn't want them to notice me if the bus hadn't arrived yet. I'd need every minute I could get.

I glanced at the sign for the schedule, then tried to check my phone.

It was dead, of course.

"Hey, what time is it?" I asked a guy sitting on the bench, scrolling on his phone.

He didn't even look at me when he answered. "Almost 7."

Looking back at the sign, I checked the sheet and did an inward victory dance. The bus would be there at 7, and then I was home-free.

My roommate Ebony and I weren't super close, but she was definitely the closest friend I had unless you counted my mom. Which I did, but most people I met did not.

Since my mom was a few hours' drive away and Ebony didn't have much family, she and I had each other's backs. We had memorized each other's phone numbers just in case of a shitty situation like the one I'd found myself dragged into.

She would definitely pick me up if I asked, but I wasn't sure I wanted to ask. I felt bad dragging her away from her schoolwork. Ebony spent even more time studying than I did, and that was saying something because I spent all of my time studying unless I was working.

We were both in nursing classes and in the same year of school, but she was in a fast-grad program that would get her out a year early. I'd applied for that one and had gotten accepted, but even with my scholarships, I couldn't afford to survive without working almost full-time at the sandwich shop.

Now that I was no longer working there, I'd have to find another job if I wanted to keep eating.

But hey, living was more important than eating, right?

"Can I use your phone to call my roommate?" I asked Phone Guy, who still hadn't glanced away from his screen.

"No."

I opened my mouth, then closed it.

He had a right to refuse me, but well, it was kind of a dick move. I didn't even have socks to cover the bandages on my bare feet, so anyone with eyes could see that I was in trouble.

The bus arrived, and a couple people got out. Every one of them glanced down at my feet as they passed, their eyebrows lifting.

My face flushed more with every person who walked by.

I stepped up to the stairs leading into the bus right behind Phone Guy. He slid a card through a little scanner thing, and I stopped.

Shit.

"Uh, do you take cash?" I asked the driver, stumbling over my words as I dug through my bag. My wallet was in there somewhere, and I probably had a couple bucks in there. I tried to always keep emergency cash on me, even if it wasn't much.

"Nope." The bus driver sounded annoyed.

I looked over my shoulder and saw an old truck fly into the sandwich shop's parking lot. Jesse's pack piled out, all of their eyes scanning the area. I didn't see Jesse, but I was confident he was in the truck somewhere.

Shit, shit, shit.

"Pay or get out," The driver barked.

Phone Guy stepped back to the scanner, and slid his card through again. A green light flashed, and the bus driver waved me on back.

I shot Phone Guy what I hoped look like a grateful look and followed him past a few full seats. Not wanting to bug him, I didn't take the seat beside his but instead sat down in the one across from it.

With a grimace, Phone Guy handed me his phone.

My throat welled. "Thank you so much."

He muttered something, and I quickly dialed Ebony's number.

Right before it went to voicemail, she answered. "Hello?"

"Hey, Ebony. It's Tea."

"Finally. Where are you? Are you okay? I thought maybe you hooked up with someone last night, but you haven't been home for your laptop. What happened?" She sounded upset, and I felt a little bad even though the kidnapping had obviously not been my fault.

"I'll explain when I get back to the dorm. Is there any way you can pick me up? I'm on a bus. The next stop is..." I scanned the sign on the wall.

"Redd street and Pope," Phone Guy muttered.

I shot him another grateful look and repeated his words.

Ebony said, "Okay, I'm leaving right now. See you soon."

After echoing the sentiment and thanking her, I handed the phone back to the guy across the aisle. "Thank you so much for everything," I told him, hoping he could tell I was being sincere.

"Yep." He looked back at his phone, turning away and ignoring me once again.

I dug through my bag until I found a wallet, and pulled out ten bucks. Though I really couldn't afford to give him anything, the guy had helped me out when he clearly didn't want to. For that, he deserved the money whether I could afford it or not.

"Thank you." I repeated, handing him the cash.

He nodded and stuck it in his pocket.

My heart stopped pounding as I settled into the seat for a minute, trying to calm myself.

The werewolves couldn't have seen me, right? They'd only been there for a moment, and I'd already been inside the bus when they got there. There was no way they'd noticed me unless they'd looked through the window, but that wasn't likely, was it?

I turned my head and watched out the window at the back of the bus. I couldn't see the truck following behind us, so that was a good sign.

When the bus stopped, I saw Ebony's car parked nearby and nearly cried in relief.

As I followed a few other people off the bus, my eyes were trained on my feet while I tried not to step on anything sharp on my way out.

The guy in front of me strode away, and I stepped down the last stair only to freeze.

Jesse sat on the ground like he was a dog rather than a wolf. Around his neck was a collar, and attached to it was a short leash that rested on the ground in a small pile of fabric.

None of the other guys were around, and I didn't see their truck or their van either.

What the hell was going on?

I tried to step past Jesse, but he got up and walked beside me like he was a dog—*my* dog. Since he could probably pass for a husky or a wolfdog to anyone who wasn't a wolf expert, I wasn't sure how I was going to get rid of him.

Tucked in his collar was a rolled-up piece of paper. I stopped, tugged it out, and unrolled it.

It read:

We talked Jesse into hunting you while you stay in school. He's going to act like any other dog. As long as you don't bring any guys home or try to escape again, he won't give you any problems. Buy him a service dog vest and no one will give you any problems either. -Elliot

I crumpled the note and tossed it in the trash can a few feet away.

"What's it going to take to get rid of you?" I asked the wolf.

He snorted.

Yeah, that was what I thought he'd say.

But what options did I really have at that point?

"Alright, fine. Let's go." I grabbed the leash off the ground and tugged him toward Ebony's car.

TEN

"YOU DITCHED SCHOOL TO BUY A DOG?" Ebony's curly black hair was up in a bun, her dark brown skin and chocolate-colored eyes framed by loose curls she'd purposefully left out. She was tall and slim, and I'd always been jealous of how long her arms were.

Yes, it was a stupid thing to be jealous about, but short arms suck.

"You don't even really like dogs," she reminded me.

Yeah, I was aware.

"I've been feeling really overwhelmed since the semester started, and my mom convinced me an emotional support dog would help," I lied. "I'll probably come to regret it, but he's trained at least."

"Where did you get the money?" Ebony frowned.

Damn smart roommate.

"Mom paid and showed up with him. She wouldn't take no for an answer." I rolled my eyes, hoping Ebony bought the story.

"What kind of dog is he?" She eyed the monster, clearly uncertain about sharing our tiny dorm room with the wolf.

"A wolfdog," I said easily. I knew that was a real type of dog, because my mom had nearly picked one of those when she decided she wanted a dog a few years back. But she'd ended up with Gallifrey, her German Shepherd, instead. And I didn't love dogs, but Gallifrey and I had developed a tenuous alliance so I had a soft spot for him. "He's trained."

I felt like shit for making crap up, but it wasn't like I could tell her Jesse was a werewolf that was hunting me because he wanted to make me into a werewolf and then make babies with me.

"Did you clear it with Madeline?" Ebony checked.

That was one thing I couldn't lie about.

"Not yet," I admitted. "I was hoping he could charm her into letting it slide."

Our dorm didn't technically allow pets, but there were a few girls with emotional support cats and small dogs. An emotional support *wolf* would be a much harder sell, but Madeline (our RA) was pretty easy-going.

"Alright, let's go." She tilted her head toward the door, still eyeing Jesse. I opened the back door, gesturing him inside.

He jumped in, and I tossed the leash in behind him before shutting it.

I sat down on my own seat, and found Ebony giving the wolf the stink-eye.

"Don't lick me," she warned.

He gave a solemn nod.

Seriously? I'd been trying to get him to quit licking me since we met.

"Did he just *nod*?" she asked.

"He was trained to do that." I spewed more bullshit. "So his owner could talk to him and feel heard."

He nodded at her again, and she laughed.

"That's actually kind of cute."

I shrugged. "I have mixed feelings about it."

She pulled away from the road. "Holy shit, Tea. What happened to your feet?"

That was going to be a harder lie to pull off.

They were wrapped up, but the bandages looked like they'd been through hell. "I took Jesse on a long walk wearing my converse, and came back with a bunch of terrible blisters," I admitted. "Threw them away in a fit of rage afterward."

She looked alarmed. "Maybe you do need a support dog."

Ouch.

"I can drive you to the sandwich shop the next few days to give you time to heal," she said.

"I actually quit." I bit my lip. "I'm looking for another job."

"Wow. Are you feeling okay?"

"Yeah. Just thought it was time to take my life into my own hands," I lied.

She didn't look convinced, but still nodded.

We reached the dorm, thankfully, and got out of the car. I grabbed Jesse's leash but didn't bother pulling on it. The wolf would follow me whether I wanted him to or not.

Our dorm was on the fourth floor, so we headed to the stairs. Ebony climbed them without a problem, leaving me in the dust as I took one slow, painful step at a time.

She came back when she realized I was way behind her. "You should go to the doctor."

"Can't afford the copay," I admitted.

That wasn't even a lie.

Her eyebrows knitted together. "How are you going to afford to feed the dog?"

I made a face. "Might have to start dancing at a strip club."

Jesse snarled.

Both of us looked at him, and he curled his mouth up to show me his fangs.

"Are you sure that's a dog?" Ebony checked.

I was sure it *wasn't* a dog.

"So says my mom," I lied.

She shrugged, and we kept going. Jesse kept growling, his side pressed up against mine.

How did I ever think he wasn't possessive?

By the time we made it to the top of the stairs, I was considering asking Jesse for a ride. But he wasn't *that* big, and I didn't want to crush him.

Though if I did, that would take care of my wolf problem...

I stopped at Madeline's door. She was only the RA for about half of the floor, since it was a mixed gender dorm. The guys on the floor had their own RA, who was kind of an asshat, but I rarely saw him so it didn't matter.

Ebony headed back to our room while I stayed to talk to Madeline. She said she had to clean a bit to make space for Jesse, but she was a neat freak. So, I knew that meant she just wanted to straighten up her desk… or avoid the uncomfortable conversation I was about to have.

I knocked on the door, and then waited. Madeline answered after a good three minutes, as always. Despite the tiny size of the dorm room, she was a music major who tended to get lost in her work and had a hard time pulling herself out of it to answer doors.

Once you had her attention though, she was all yours.

"Oh hell." She stared at the wolf, not bothering with a greeting. Her eyes lifted to mine after a minute. "Tea..." she warned.

"He's an emotional support dog," I offered. "He knows lots of tricks. Jesse, sit," I commanded without so much as glancing at him.

He sat.

"He's huge." Madeline shoved a hand through her wavy, platinum-blonde hair. "Sterling's going to throw a fit."

Sterling was the asshat, and he and Madeline had to agree on stuff that affected the whole floor.

"Jesse, spin," I ordered, hoping to show her that he was obedient.

He gave me a dry stare but then he slowly spun around.

"Look, he's a big sweetheart. My mom's an overbearing single mother, and she's worried about me. She found this guy and brought him to me, and wouldn't take no for an answer." I tried to appeal to Madeline's empathetic side. Squatting down, I wrapped my arms around Jesse's neck to cuddle him just so I could make a statement. He licked my cheek, then my nose, and then my neck. "See?" I looked pointedly at her.

She sighed. "I'll go talk to Sterling. I can't make any promises, though. You know he's an ass."

"I know. Thanks, Del." I gave her a big smile and used her nickname just to sweeten her up, releasing the wolf and straightening. He licked my wrist, and I resisted the urge to lecture him again.

"You're lucky I'm so cool," she reminded me.

"I know." I gave her a quick hug before heading down the hall a few doors, to my room.

Ebony was sitting at her desk, already buried in a video about anatomy again. She was in the same second-year anatomy class I was taking, and the damn thing was hell for our minds. There was so much memorizing to do, and that made it a struggle just to stay sane while spending so much time trying to embed the names of bones and muscles in my brain.

Our room was pretty simple. White walls, brown carpet flooring. We'd thought about putting a rug on the floor, but all of the ones we'd both liked were even more expensive than our textbooks, so we'd decided we loved the color brown.

My twin bed was fairly tall, made of a light yellowish wood that I didn't love but didn't hate either, and the dresser was built into the bottom of the bed. All of the clothes stuffed into the dresser had come from thrift stores, same as the pink and gray floral-patterned comforter I'd had since I was twelve.

My mom and I had survived off a high school teacher's salary, so we used things until they wore out.

My desk was at the end of my bed, and I could tell Ebony had straightened up my books, papers, and laptop. We'd reached a truce ages ago. She didn't complain about my messy desk, as long as I didn't complain if she organized it when it bothered her.

Ebony's bed was across from mine. It was a loft bed, with the desk and a small set of drawers both built in underneath the raised mattress. She'd offered that bed to me on the first day we moved in, but I could tell she wanted it. And I didn't particularly like the idea of waking up and smashing my head into our short ceiling in the process, so I didn't have a problem telling her it was all hers.

Jesse hopped up on my bed without bothering to ask if it was mine. Given that he was, you know, a wolf, I was sure he could smell me on it.

Digging into my bottom dresser, I found the small first-aid kit I'd put together before moving into my dorm. I set it on the bed and unzipped it, rifling through. Luckily, I found some gauze pads and a roll of medical tape, plus some antibiotic ointment.

It was a little ironic that I was a nursing student who didn't actually know how to deal with injuries, but I was just barely starting my second year. All I'd really taken was the basic classes and an intro to nursing course that was meant to scare students into abandoning their degree in favor of something easier.

Grabbing the supplies, I told Jesse to stay there and hobbled to the bathroom.

To my surprise, he stayed.

I rinsed my feet, dropping enough curse words to make the damn wolf blush as I tried to clean the wounds. They were looking worse than they had before, which didn't strike me as a great sign. But it was my fault, since I'd been walking on them.

After rebandaging them, I hobbled back to the dorm and grabbed some thick socks out of my top drawer. I pulled them on, then looked between my desk and the bed.

My feet were throbbing, and I was pretty sure elevation would help them.

But the wolf was on my bed, and there wasn't much other space for him to sit. Ebony wouldn't like him sitting on the ground for long, and he'd be a tripping hazard.

With an inward groan, I grabbed my laptop and slipped up onto the bed. The wolf made space for me, but it wasn't a big bed. Our sides pressed together as I opened my computer.

I sent off a few emails to my professors, apologizing for missing class and claiming a family emergency that I knew my mom would back up if asked. I turned in assignments I was supposed to have in hours earlier, and then pulled up the same anatomy video Ebony had been watching and taking notes on.

The video was boring. I set it on double-speed, and got comfortable in the bed. I hadn't eaten dinner and it was already nine PM, but food would've required getting up and leaving, which I didn't want to do. So, I stayed in bed.

I found myself snuggling up to the wolf while I pulled my blanket up to my chest and watched the video. I typed notes into the document I had pulled up on the bottom of the screen every now and then, but I was so exhausted that I was having a hard time focusing.

My eyes grew heavy when Jesse ducked his head under the blanket, cuddling up against my legs. My leggings stayed on and kept his fur from tickling me, which he didn't seem to mind one bit. The old familiar comforter and Jesse's body heat lulled me to sleep halfway through the video.

I jerked awake a few hours later to a knock at the door. Something wet was on my chin, so I lifted my hand. When I pulled my hand away and found drool, I cringed.

Ebony opened the door, revealing an annoyed-looking Madeline.

"Hey, ladies." She gave us a grimace that told me she was going to say something I didn't like. "I've got bad news."

Crap.

I rubbed at my eyes, and she came the rest of the way inside. Ebony shut the door behind her.

"I've been arguing with Sterling for hours, but he won't budge. Jesse can't stay. He's big enough to be considered a threat to safety and property." Her eyes were apologetic. "You have forty-eight hours to find another home for the dog, or to find another place to live."

ELEVEN

"FORTY-EIGHT HOURS?" I repeated.

"I'm sure your mom can take him back to wherever she found him," Ebony offered.

If he was actually a dog, that would've worked.

Given that he was a hunting werewolf, I was thinking it was a no-go.

"I'll call her tomorrow," I managed to say, glancing at the clock. It was almost midnight; she was definitely asleep.

"Sorry. I even called my advisor, but she agreed with Sterling," Madeline apologized. "There's a twenty-pound limit."

"Thanks for trying." I wrapped my arms around my stomach. "I really appreciate it."

"That's what I'm here for." She gave me a sad smile. "He does seem like a good dog."

Of course he did; he wanted me to be his wolfy wife.

"Have a good night," Madeline said, stepping out of the room.

"Dammit," I muttered.

"Now you have an excuse to give your mom," Ebony offered.

My forced smile was brittle.

If only it was that simple.

"I'm going to go to bed and figure it out in the morning," I mumbled. "Goodnight."

Turning over, I accidentally ended up cuddling the wolf.

He licked the top of my foot, and I was too tired to tell him off for it. Or to roll away from him.

So I just shut my eyes, and went to sleep.

SINCE I FORGOT to plug in my phone, my alarm didn't go off, and I didn't wake up until noon the next day. Jesse was still exactly where I'd left him. My feet were throbbing even worse than they'd been the day before, and I knew I had an assload of homework and studying to catch up on.

Ebony was already in class; her classes were spread out on every day of the week, with gaps between each of them so she had time to study after every class to really let the material sink in. She was living my dream life, with her fast-grad program and her study time.

But I was surviving.

Mostly.

I wiggled my laptop out from underneath the wolf. It had been sandwiched between us when I rolled over the night before, and I hadn't even noticed.

Jesse licked my ankle.

"Don't push your luck," I mumbled.

He licked again.

The obvious tease reminded me of Jesse in the sandwich shop, before his wolf had taken over. He'd made a joke—the veggie sandwich joke.

Honestly, it had been a little funny.

I opened my laptop and pulled up a blank document. Lists weren't really my thing, but sometimes they could help me organize my thoughts.

"Alright. I have forty-eight hours to find a new place, or get rid of you," I spoke to Jesse.

Why I was speaking to him at all was beyond me, but I typed 48 HOURS at the top of my page. Beneath that, I typed out the two options: get rid of Jesse, and find a new place.

"The simplest option would be to get rid of you. Can you leave?" I checked.

He growled at me.

"That'll be a no. Second simplest option would be to move into your house." I paused. "Or your human's house? I don't know how to talk about you two. Or you one. Werewolves are weird."

He blew a puff of air on my ankle, and I kicked at him on instinct. That earned me a wolfy chuckle and another puff of air.

"But I don't have a car, so I have no way to get there," I said, adding that to my document. "I'd have to walk, since I also don't have phone numbers for any of your buddies. I guess you could go retrieve one of them, but I'm not sure I can talk you into leaving my side..."

I bit my lip, focusing on typing out all the potential problems with my plan.

The wolf was lapping at my ankle like it was a damn water bowl at that point, but I was getting over it.

"If we did go with that plan, I could probably take your car to my classes on the days I have class. I can't get my money back for the semester, but if I freeze most of the shit in your fridge and ration it, I might have the food and funds to survive the next couple of months. Gas money would be hard to swing, but with the food in the freezer..." I trailed off as I continued typing. "Plus, you can hunt for food since you're a wolf and all, so I don't have to feed you if I stay there."

When I finished typing, I moved to option two.

"Or, I can get rid of you. But you already said you won't leave, so the only way to really do that is by asking you to bite me, right?" I checked.

His tongue paused on my inner-ankle and his teeth scraped my leg. I shivered.

That would be a yes.

"Assuming I let you bite me, I either die, or you go back to human form." I didn't ask that time, not wanting another nibble to confirm it.

He nibbled confirmation anyway.

"And if I survive, I become a werewolf."

Another nibble on my ankle answered that question.

My fingers were slow as I typed that out.

I was already leaning toward option one.

"Assuming I move back to your place, how much time would that buy me? A week? A month? A year?"

The wolf resumed licking.

"I should've gotten Ford's phone number," I muttered. "Alright, I need an answer to that question. Nod for yes, shake your head for no." I lifted the blanket off his head.

He ignored me, continuing to lick my ankle.

"I'm not kidding, Jesse. I can't make a decision unless you at least give me an estimate." He continued licking. "How long do most people get after the wolf starts hunting before they get bitten? I'm going to rattle off timeframes, and you nibble when I get to the average, okay?"

He didn't acknowledge me, but I knew he'd heard me. And he seemed to like nibbling on me, so I assumed he'd be cool with it.

"A week," I said.

No nibble.

"Two weeks."

No nibble.

"Three weeks?"

Nothing.

"A month."

Just more licking.

"Two months?" I asked.

That time, he hesitated.

"Three months?"

He nibbled, then.

"Two to three months. Wow, that's longer than I expected. I can work with three months."

I did the math mentally. We were almost to the end of September, so three months would get me to Christmas.

Of course, three months was probably the average timeframe. Which meant Jesse might give me more time, or less time. It couldn't be an exact science, or else the wolf wouldn't be *hunting*, he would just be *waiting*.

"Let's make a deal," I told the wolf.

His tongue paused on my ankle.

"If you let me finish the semester out and spend one last Christmas with my mom before you bite me, I'll stop fighting you."

It wouldn't be Stockholm Syndrome, because I was no longer a victim.

At least, I didn't think I was a victim. It was hard to say, given the strange, supernatural position I'd somehow managed to land myself in.

But victim or not, I had to deal with the hand I'd been dealt. And I'd been dealt a *werewolf*.

The wolf finally lifted his head, looking in my eyes.

"I'll even be *nice* to you," I added. "If I'm going to die when you bite me, I want to die having finished the semester...

and my mom loves Christmas, so I want to spend it with her so she has good memories of me. If I don't die, I can start the spring semester back up without a problem."

Jesse stared at me.

I stared back.

He finally nodded his head.

"Thank you," I said.

He licked my ankle.

I deleted the document I'd typed up, so there was no evidence of my werewolf notes or anything, and got out of bed to go use the bathroom. I'd been needing to pee since I woke up, but was dreading the walk there.

My feet hurt even more than they had the day before.

Stopping before I headed down the hallway, I pulled some ibuprofen out of my dresser and grabbed an old water bottle off the window ledge, swallowing the meds. After opening my dresser and pulling out the first pair of clean clothes I saw, I finally shuffled toward the bathroom.

Jesse didn't stay in bed that time. But he did walk beside me, and it was nice to have him there so I could use him to break my fall if the pain got too bad and I crashed.

He waited for me outside while I peed and changed. I was in too much pain to even take the time to brush my damn teeth, so minty gum would save my mouth.

After we walked back, he gave me a stern look and a warning growl before he slipped out the door.

He probably needed to go, too, and was trying to tell me not to leave.

I peeked out the window, and a minute later, watched the wolf trot out onto the lawn outside the dorm. He ignored the gaping, pointing humans, disappearing out of my view and probably theirs too.

When ten minutes had passed and he didn't return, I was a bit concerned.

When twenty minutes had passed and he was still gone, I wondered if he'd ran into a bear while taking a piss.

Opening my computer, I focused on typing bullshit answers for my English 301 class assignment, while glancing back and forth at the clock every now and then.

An hour and a half had passed when the wolf finally scratched at the door. I got out of bed and pulled it open, then stepped back when I found Ford in the doorway beside Jesse.

"Your ride has arrived," he said with a small grin.

TWELVE

"I'M surprised you sent the wolf after us so soon, considering how much convincing we had to do to get him into that collar," Ford said. He sniffed the air. "Why does it smell so good in here?"

"Probably because you're used to hanging out with men," I said before I stepped backward, sitting down on the edge of my bed to get off my feet.

Ford shrugged.

Jesse wormed his way into my small closet, and came back dragging a massive rolling suitcase in his teeth.

"My RA said he can't stay," I explained to Ford. "Me and Jesse made a deal. He's going to let me finish out the semester before biting me, in exchange for me living at his house, driving his car."

Ford barked out a laugh. "You're getting the raw end of that deal, Teagan."

"I go by Tea," I told him. "And I know, but I'm trying to deal with the shitshow my life has become thanks to you bastards."

I grabbed the massive suitcase from Jesse and tugged it up onto my bed. After I unzipped the thing, I pulled out the smaller suitcase inside it and handed it to Ford. "Can you grab everything out of my closet and put it in here?"

"Mmhm." He headed to the closet.

Jesse grabbed a mouthful of my clothes and lifted them up onto the bed. I made a face, shoving them into my suitcase. "Thanks, Jesse, but I'd rather not get everything I own wet with wolf slobber."

He licked my ankle, and I eased myself back down to my feet.

That Ibuprofen really needed to kick in already.

Moving everything from my dresser to the suitcases was fast and easy. I didn't fold it; that could wait until my feet didn't hurt so damn much.

When that was done, I started grabbing everything else I owned and throwing it in the suitcase too. I didn't own anything nice; even my laptop was one of the cheapest functional models. College was about surviving, so that I wouldn't have to worry about money afterward.

I couldn't wait to not have to stress about money. I'd be able to buy my mom the things she'd never bought herself growing up, because we couldn't afford it back then. Hardcover books and candles were some of her favorite things on the planet, and they weren't even expensive, but they'd been an unnecessary expense we couldn't fit in the budget for as long as I could remember. After I graduated, we'd live close to each other and I could drop off presents randomly to let her know that she was loved.

Ford and I packed up my life quickly. My phone was *still* dead, so I scribbled a note on a sheet of paper to let Ebony know I was moving out with my new "dog" and that I'd text her when I got my phone charged.

Walking down to Ford's car was painful, but when we made it, I took the passenger seat and lifted my feet up to rest on the dashboard while Jesse jumped into the back seat. I was surprised Ford's sports car had a back seat, but then again, it seemed like their pack spent a lot of time together, so he probably needed the extra seats.

Ford opened his mouth to tell me to take my feet off the dash, but Jesse leaned forward between the seats and growled at Ford.

The man shut his mouth, pulling his sports car away from my school. He turned music on, and I shut my eyes and cursed the throbbing in my feet. I really wasn't doing the damn things any favors by walking around, but what else was there to do?

Ford and I didn't say much to each other on the drive back to Moon Ridge. Jesse's head remained between us at all times—probably a result of my unethical escape. I knew I should probably apologize to Ford for kissing him and the others, but I couldn't even remember if he was one of the guys I'd kissed.

The whole escape was a blur, and I really didn't feel bad about it. I'd been kidnapped, and then I'd escaped. It didn't seem all that complicated to me, even though the way I went about escaping was questionable.

Ford parked in front of Jesse's house, which seemed like a polite gesture. He helped me carry my bags inside, and at the wolf's insistence, carried the suitcases up to Jesse's bedroom.

I wasn't going to sleep in Jesse-the-guy's bed, but I guess that was a nice gesture too.

Ford met me back in the kitchen, where I was scavenging for more Ibuprofen and some Tylenol too. He gestured to the corner of the counter. "We put Jesse's phone on the charger over there yesterday."

I glanced over. The exact same phone I had was sitting plugged into a charger. It had a plain black case on it, and my case was purple, so I knew Ford was right that was Jesse's.

Ford added, "The code to the phone and the garage is twelve-twelve. The same code works for the rest of our packs' garages and phones too. We all have access to each other's homes, and spare car keys and shit, so if you're ever locked out just knock on one of our doors."

He slid his hands into his pockets. "Our numbers are all in Jesse's phone. His parents' are too. Call any of us, or them, if you need anything. We know getting chosen by a wolf isn't ideal, and we want to help you however we can."

He paused, watching my reaction. I didn't react; what would I do or say? When I didn't do or say anything, he continued. "Jesse's got a mate-cash-stash on top of his fridge. We all have them. It's supposed to help you out while we're stuck in wolf form. Jesse's not a guy who would abandon you to figure this shit out yourself, so don't hold it against him that his wolf is in control right now."

He waited for my reaction once again, but once again, I didn't react. "Everyone in the pack has dinner together almost every night, as you know. You don't have to join us, but it's free food. We'll text the meal rotation to Jesse's phone in case you want to. I think that's about everything." He eased his way toward the door. "If you have any questions, just text or call one of us. Or walk over."

"Thanks," I said, a little overwhelmed by everything he'd told me.

"No problem." He ducked out the door, closing it behind him. It shut, and then opened again immediately. "I forgot to tell you, make sure you lock the doors at night. You're not in danger here, but Jesse will be easier to deal with at night if the doors are locked."

I nodded. He hadn't seemed difficult the night before, but I'd keep it in mind.

With that, Ford did leave.

I glanced at the wolf. He was sitting on the ground beside me, just watching me.

"What's a mate-cash-stash?" I asked him.

He tilted his head.

I pulled a chair over to the fridge, too curious not to. It sounded like he'd been storing money for his mate, but that couldn't be right. Who would save money for a stranger?

Climbing up the chair, I peeked over the top of the fridge. Sure enough, there was a thick envelope up there. I grabbed it, then carefully stepped down from the chair and up to the counter. The envelope wasn't sealed, so I just opened the flap and tugged out money.

It wasn't just money—it was a stack of money. A *massive* stack of money.

I flipped through the stack, shock blooming within me. The bottom half was hundred-dollar-bills; the top half was fifties. Altogether, there was at least five thousand dollars.

I dropped the money on the countertop. My eyes flicked back to the envelope, and I noticed writing on it that I hadn't seen before.

I picked it up. Words were scribbled on it in black ink.

It took a minute of squinting for me to decipher the messy handwriting, but I did. It said:

For my mate: I'm sorry you've been dragged into my world. Hopefully this helps ease your transition. Use it on food, or clothes, or whatever. It's yours.

I dropped the envelope, shaking my head.

Leaving money for the mate you knew your wolf would insist on hunting was something a good person would do. But that went against almost everything I'd been thinking since the abduction.

Jesse the human couldn't be a good guy. He just... couldn't. His friends had abducted me. He was a werewolf, for crying out loud. Werewolves kidnapped people, and ignored women screaming for help as they were dragged to their captors' homes.

Sure, they were also friendly when you asked for directions, and they would offer to turn up the AC if you started stripping, but they weren't good people.

Were they?

I rubbed my head. A headache was building, even with the ibuprofen and Tylenol in my system.

I needed sleep, and a hearty dose of reality.

Shoving the money back into the envelope, I stuck it back on top of the fridge and dragged the chair back to the kitchen table.

Though I needed sleep, I had to do my homework. I had a test for my chemistry class that closed on Saturday, so I also needed to study my ass off.

What I really needed was an energy drink.

I tugged open Jesse's fridge. It was still filled nearly to explosion with food, but there were no energy drinks. With a sigh, I grabbed the bag of leftover pizza before heading to the stairs. My laptop bag was in my big suitcase, which meant it was in Jesse's room.

The wolf walked slowly up the stairs beside me, capturing the bag of pizza between his teeth and carrying it up the stairs for me.

"This is going to be a long day," I warned him, as we reached the top. "All I have time for is studying."

He dropped the pizza bag on the ground next to my suitcase and licked my wrist.

"Guess you don't care what we do, huh?" I asked him.

He blew a puff of air on my wrist, and I absentmindedly scratched him behind the ear with my spare hand as I unzipped my suitcase.

I caught myself petting him a moment later and jerked my hand away.

What the hell was I doing?

The werewolves were going to make me lose my damn mind.

How was I supposed to prevent it, though?

THIRTEEN

MY PHONE'S alarm went off early, since I had to get up in time to drive to the campus for my classes. Fridays were always the longest day of the week for me, even though I had the same Friday schedule on Mondays and Wednesdays too.

My face jerked up off the carpeted floor of Jesse's room, and I looked around blearily. I hadn't meant to fall asleep there.

Jesse licked my face, and I groaned.

My tired fingers struggled with the zippers on my suitcases. When I finally got them open, I grabbed the first clothes I touched and got dressed awkwardly on the floor.

I was starting to wonder if my feet would ever heal.

Obviously that was a bit dramatic, but the pain was horrible, and I couldn't avoid walking.

I put on my athletic shoes before shuffling to the bathroom to do my hair.

A few minutes later, with my hair in a messy ponytail and dark circles beneath my eyes, I made my way down the stairs. Makeup was the last thing on my mind. As long as I wasn't naked or stinky, I looked good enough for my classes.

Jesse walked beside me, keeping my pace until we reached the kitchen. He licked my leg—which was mostly bare, thanks to the flowy blue shorts I wore with a white tank tucked into them.

After swallowing pain meds, I grabbed Jesse's car keys off their hook. Someone had put them back since I'd been there last; probably whoever plugged his phone in.

Jesse barked, and I looked over at him. He was crouched in front of the fridge door.

"You're hungry?" I asked.

He shook his head.

"Why else would you bark at the fridge?"

My stomach took that moment to rumble.

He looked pointedly at me, and I realized he was growling because he wanted me to eat.

That was thoughtful, in a wolfy way. I was sure wolves shared food, so him telling me to eat before I left was pretty much the same as a wolf proudly nudging me toward an animal carcass and telling me, "The first bite's yours!"

"Thanks, but I don't usually eat breakfast. Two meals a day costs less than three. I'll drink some water on the way there," I told the wolf.

He growled.

I put a hand on my hip. "I just quit my job and moved to a place where I need to have gas money. There's about three hundred bucks in my bank account right now, and the semester just started. That means I've got a hundred bucks a month for both gas and food, so unless *you're* going to go out and get a job, two meals a day is going to have to cut it."

I hadn't seen any disposable water bottles in the pantry, so I went to the cupboard I'd found cups in. On the top shelf, there were a couple of water bottles laying on their sides. I pulled one out and filled it up, waving it toward the wolf pointedly.

Jesse barked again. He lifted his head toward the top of the fridge, and I knew he was pointing at the money up there.

"I'm not spending money that belongs to someone I've never met. If I'm between starving and spending his money, I'll go out and get a new job. Don't know how I'll work it with you following me everywhere, but I'll figure it out."

I headed toward the garage. Jesse whined but followed me out.

Jesse's car had me lifting my eyebrows when I saw it. Not because it was expensive or anything—because it was the exact same car my mom had driven for the past ten years.

A silver Honda Civic.

I hadn't really noticed it the last time I was out there, but now that I had, it was impossible to ignore. It looked like it might even be the same year as my mom's, which was fifteen years old.

The paint was faded and the windshield had a crack running along the bottom of it. Most people would've been turned off by that, but to me, that made me feel more comfortable. I would've felt awkward driving an expensive car when my laptop and phone were the only things I owned that had cost more than ten bucks.

Except during a getaway, like when I'd driven Ford's sports car.

I'd only been thinking about my survival, then.

The wolf followed me to the car. When I opened the driver's side door, he slipped inside and jumped over to the passenger seat.

Guess he was going to school with me.

"You won't be allowed in the classes," I warned.

He snorted.

Did that mean he'd already known that, or that he was going to shove his way inside anyway?

I hoped it was the former. Otherwise, someone was bound to get suspicious of the "wolfdog".

There was a button clipped to the visor, and I recognized it as a garage button so I pressed it. The garage door raised, and I backed out. Just the pressure of my foot on the gas pedal hurt.

Hopefully the pain meds would kick in soon.

Two of Jesse's friends were outside, shirtless, and tossing a football back and forth. I was pretty sure their names were Rocco and Elliot.

Maybe they were a football team after all.

They waved as I passed. I debated not waving back out of principle since the assholes had kidnapped me, but that felt unnecessary, so I just waved back.

My stomach growled as I sipped my water. Jesse growled back at it.

"I'm fine. It'll stop," I told the wolf.

He huffed.

Both my stomach and Jesse continued to growl at each other throughout the drive to my school. When I got there, I passed a sign about parking permits.

"Shit," I mumbled.

I hadn't considered a parking pass. They were expensive. My mom and I had talked about the insane price of parking when I first decided I'd go to school there. The price was more than I had in my whole damn bank account, at the moment.

My eyes landed on a parking meter—easier than a permit, and a temporary solution. It was eight bucks for all day parking. Eight times three, for three days a week of parking, times four for four weeks a month, times three for three months...

Shit.

Shit, shit, shit.

Almost three hundred bucks.

Maybe the local animal shelter was hiring.

Maybe someone wanted to buy a *wolfdog*.

I glanced at Jesse.

Unfortunately, even I wasn't cruel enough to sic him on someone else.

Sliding my debit card, I considered just going ahead and telling the wolf to bite me. It would sure save me an assload of stress if I died instead of changing.

But I wasn't ready to die, so that was off the table.

I grabbed my bag out of the back seat and headed toward the building that held my first class. Jesse trotted beside me. Everyone we passed stared at him, or tried to pet him.

He dodged their hands, remaining at my side.

"Most dogs like being petted," I whispered.

He shot me a dark look. I thought it might translate to something along the lines of, *"As you previously pointed out multiple times, I'm not a dog."*

He'd liked it when I scratched his head the night before though, so I knew it wasn't that he didn't like being touched...

Or maybe he only liked being touched by me, because he was hunting me to be his mate.

Yikes.

"I have two classes in this building. I'll be out in about two and a half hours, and then I'll head to a building over there," I told Jesse, pointing across the campus in the direction of my third class. "I don't have a lunch break or anything. My classes are all back-to-back, so we can meet at the car at six if you want. That's when I'll be done."

A guy walking past me shot me a strange look. I waved at him, and he looked away.

Yeah, most dogs couldn't understand times. I wasn't even sure Jesse could.

He licked my knee.

"If I don't see you there, I'll assume you ran back to Moon Ridge," I warned.

He licked my knee again, and then licked the other one.

Weirdo.

"Alright. Well, bye." I gave the wolf an awkward pat on the head and went inside to my first class.

The first and second ones were my most boring classes. I sat through them, yawning frequently and struggling to focus on anything but my throbbing feet. I needed stronger pain meds.

When I headed out to my third class, I assumed Jesse would already be gone. I was surprised to find him lying on the ground just outside the door. Some girl was babbling to him, petting his head.

He didn't look happy about it.

When he saw me, he jumped up and shook out his fur. After shooting the girl beside him a look of disdain, he trotted up to me and licked the inside of my knee. I screeched and pretty much jumped away.

The sidewalk was flooded with people, so when I jumped away, I slammed into some guy. His hands landed on my waist as he steadied me before I could fall over.

Tall and slim, with stylish glasses and a Star Wars t-shirt, he was attractive in my favorite way: smart-hot.

"I'm so sorry," I apologized.

He gave me a crooked grin. "It's fine. I'd probably scream if a dog that big licked my knee too."

Yeah, definitely my type.

I didn't glance back at the wolf. He saw me as his mate, but I was only staying with him to save my damn life.

I could get this guy's number and text him until things were over with the werewolves, right? Granted, I might be a werewolf when it was over...

Which I really didn't want to think about.

I knew I should probably walk away from the cute nerd, but I'd already run into him. I had an excuse.

"Do you want to go out sometime?" I blurted. "I mean, I kind of owe you for smashing into you."

I knew that with smart-hot guys, I had to take the initiative. Even if he was interested, he likely wouldn't have the guts to make the first move, if he realized I wanted to go out with him at all.

Jesse snarled.

Me and the cute nerd glanced over at the wolf just in time to see him shove his way between our bodies.

Shit. Right. Possessive.

Jesse snapped his teeth at the hot nerd, and the hottie jumped away. "Someone should call animal control," he said, eyeing Jesse.

"Sorry, uh, this is actually my dog." I patted Jesse on the head a little harder than I needed to. "He's... *protective*."

The wolf snarled an agreement.

"Wow." The guy didn't look impressed, but he did lift his eyes back to me. "I'd love to go out with you. How about dinner, tonight?"

Free food *and* attractive company I could talk about Star Wars with?

Um, yes.

"That sounds great." I gave him a quick smile.

"What's your number?" he asked, pulling out his phone.

Jesse snarled a third time. He took a threatening step toward the hot nerd, but the guy barely batted an eye at the wolf now that he knew he was my "dog".

I quickly gave him my phone number, my fingers wrapping around Jesse's collar. "I've got to go to class, but I'm looking forward to it." I gave him a quick smile. "See you tonight."

I guess that last statement pushed the wolf over the edge.

Jesse launched toward the hot nerd, his teeth open and aimed at the guy's throat.

FOURTEEN

MY FINGERS WERE STILL WRAPPED around Jesse's collar, so I yanked on it at the same time that I tackled him. We hit the asphalt road hard, rolling a couple times.

Jesse stopped fighting the moment we collided with the ground, but his chest was heaving and I'd never seen his creepy red eyes so furious.

When we stopped rolling, I groaned. I was on top of him, sprawled out with my poor limbs scratched and bleeding.

"Are you okay?" the hot nerd asked, crouching beside me.

"Peachy." I winced as I climbed off Jesse's furry body.

My life had become so much more painful since I met those freakin' werewolves.

The hot nerd reached for me, to help me up, and Jesse lunged toward him again.

"Dammit, Jesse!" I grabbed his collar again, wrapping my arms around his neck and holding on with every ounce of muscle I had. "Leave the nice man alone." I shot the hottie a desperate look. "I'm so sorry."

"Are you sure you don't want me to call animal control?" he checked.

"I'm sure. Jesse's going to behave," I shot him a glare. "Right?"

He glared back at me.

I remembered Ford's warning... that as long as I didn't bring any guys home, Jesse was supposed to behave.

"I've got to get to class. I'll see you tonight." The guy gave me a tentative smile before walking away.

"I'm not going to sleep with him," I hissed at the wolf. "You're not dating me; we're not together. You're a freaking *wolf*. Back the hell off."

Jesse snarled at me, and then attacked.

Not with his teeth; I didn't think he'd bite me, regardless of what I did, until he wanted to change me.

He attacked me with his *tongue*.

He licked my face, and my neck, and my arms, and my clothes, and my legs. Even as I sputtered and tried to push him away, he kept licking me.

"I've got to go to class." I shoved at his face when he continued licking. "Stop it; I get that you think I'm yours."

"Your dog is so cute!" another girl exclaimed, kneeling beside me. "It's so sweet that he loves you so much."

I bit back a snort.

At least one of us thought so.

"Is he a wolfdog?" she asked.

Uh-oh. Girl knew her dogs.

"Yep. He's been through a lot of training though—even if it doesn't seem like it sometimes."

"That was just him being protective," the girl cooed at the wolf. "Isn't that right?"

He shot me a dark look.

I returned it with an identical, though human, expression.

"Well, I've got to go to class. My dog just sort of hangs out while I'm here, so feel free to hang on to him for a bit," I said, trying to slip away.

Jesse shook the girl off immediately. It made her laugh, but she stepped back.

"I'll let you go," she promised him. "Have a good day."

"You too." I hurried down the sidewalk, wincing with every damn step.

A few of the cuts and scrapes on my arms and legs were bleeding. Jesse noticed, and licked one. For once, I ignored the licking.

He let me go to class, and I spent the entirety of the lecture trying to come up with a way to escape the wolf.

But once again, I couldn't come up with a damn thing.

Jesse waited outside for me after every class. I tried exiting through different doors than the ones I'd come inside through, I tried slipping away in crowds of people, and I even tried *running* after one of my classes.

Everywhere I went, the wolf tailed me.

I had to admit he was good. Whether it was his sense of smell that made him that way, or he just had really good ears and could hear me wherever I was, I didn't know.

The hot nerd texted me partway through the day. His name was Kevin, and he said he'd pick me up at 8. My feet were throbbing and I had a shit ton of studying to do, but I didn't want to cancel after the mess with Jesse on the sidewalk earlier.

I wasn't sure how I was going to pull the date off with the wolf tailing me, but I'd figure it out.

When I got back to Jesse's place, I opened the fridge. I hadn't had anything to eat all day, and my stomach felt like it was carving itself.

I needed to go through the food and freeze a bunch of stuff to make it last, but that could wait until tomorrow.

Since I wasn't sure if yogurt froze well or not, I grabbed a container of it and a spoon, sliding up on the counter. I propped my feet up, tilting my head back at the relief and pain that hit together.

"I should stay home tonight," I told myself and Jesse, thinking about Kevin.

The wolf growled his agreement, jumping up on the counter and sitting beside me. He didn't fit, but he didn't seem to care.

His head lowered to rest on my thigh. I was at the point where I didn't even really mind it anymore—probably a sign of Stockholm Syndrome.

It was terrible, but I didn't really mind that either.

I was alive, and I had a hot date planned, and I had a place to live. And for the time being, I had food to eat too.

My eyes drifted to the envelope on top of the fridge.

If I wanted, I could have food to eat for the rest of the semester.

But spending Jesse's money would be a dick move on my part, and I wasn't a dick.

At least, not usually.

I decided I wouldn't spend his money unless I accepted that we were mates. And since I doubted that would ever happen, the envelope would stay firmly on top of the fridge until Jesse the guy was in the wolf's place. He could spend the money to upgrade his phone and car if that was what he wanted.

"Wait..." I stopped eating my yogurt, staring at the wolf. He blinked at me. "What happens after you turn back into a guy? Say you bite me and I become a werewolf... Ford said there will be lust, but we can ignore some horniness. Will I be able to leave, if I want?"

The wolf neither confirmed nor denied the statement. He closed his eyes, and a few seconds later, his breathing evened out as he fell asleep. Or pretended to fall asleep.

Dammit, I hated when he pretended he was all animal.

I stretched my arms, reaching past the wolf to grab Jesse's phone off the charger. I hadn't planned on picking it up, but I definitely needed to know what exactly was going to happen after Wolf Jesse bit me.

I called Ford first, and he didn't answer. Mentally, I went through the other guys whose names I remembered.

Zed...too bad-boy-esque.

Elliot...too happy.

Rocco...lighthearted and easily embarrassed.

Perfect.

He picked up on the first ring. "Hello?"

"Hi, Rocco. It's Tea," I said.

There was a moment of silence.

Did he seriously not remember kidnapping me, and then being kissed by me?

"Teagan Foch? Wolf Jesse thinks I'm his mail-order bride minus the mail-order and all of my personal feelings on the matter? You can't really have forgotten helping abduct me from the sandwich shop."

"I didn't forget," he agreed. "I'm just suspicious about why you're calling."

"That's fair." I scratched my head. "Ford said I could call any of you if I had questions about the werewolf shit."

He let out a breath. Maybe he was worried I was going to proposition him or something. "Yeah, totally. Any time."

"So after the wolf bites me, assuming I survive, does the hunt end?" I checked. "Will Jesse let me out of his sight again?"

"The hunt ends after you're changed," Rocco agreed. He paused again, though.

"But..." I prodded.

"But after the hunt, comes the chase."

FIFTEEN

"THE CHASE?" My voice raised an octave.

"Yeah."

"What the hell is the chase? All Ford told me was that we'd be horny in our human forms."

"Nature draws wolves to their mates after they've chosen. The hunt starts when a guy's wolf picks a girl, and ends when he's marked her as his, permanently. The chase is the female wolf's process of choosing her mate."

"A male wolf's hunt is predictable; he pretty much just follows his woman around until he bites her. The length of time it takes is the only thing that's really up in the air. Female wolves are completely unpredictable. She tests her mate until she believes he's a good choice in both human and wolf form. When she's made up her mind, she bites him, and the chase ends."

"Tell me there's not a third phase." I smacked a hand to my forehead.

"The third is the last one. It's called the climax," he said sheepishly.

"What is it?"

"Exactly what it sounds like. Lots and lots of sex."

I groaned. "That's the lust Ford was talking about, then."

"Yeah. It's supposed to be damn near impossible to do or think about anything else."

I figured I'd better get as much information as I could and face all the facts at once, so I continued with the questions. "After the lust ends, then what?"

"Then the wolves are mated permanently. They'll never so much as look at anyone else. You and Jesse could live separately if you wanted, but your wolves will find each other every time they get the chance. Your lives will be easier if you fall in love," Rocco explained.

Well, that was shitty.

"So if I, say, had a date tonight..." I trailed off. "I don't, of course. But if I did, what exactly would happen?"

"If Jesse thinks he's going to lose you, he'll bite you. Period. The wolf won't let his mate get away without marking her. Even if your wolf doesn't choose his, he's going to bind himself to you permanently. Jesse's our pack's omega, so he's the most laid-back and independent guy in the group, but a hunting wolf can only take so much."

"Would you want to be on wolf-watching duty, then?" I asked. "I can pay in yogurt and lunch meat."

Rocco snorted. "I hope you're joking. If Jesse had been anything but an omega, your little stunt the other day would've ripped our damn pack apart and ended his hunt. There's not a chance in hell I'm going to risk my family so you can go out with some dick."

I sighed.

"Cancel the date, Tea. I can understand wanting to push boundaries, but that's a hell of a lot more than pushing. The wolf considers you married, and he's an animal. You come home smelling like some other guy, he will hunt that guy down and kill him."

Rocco's lecture continued. "Even if nothing happens, Jesse's no dummy. He can hear you; he knows you're planning a date. If he's acting relaxed right now, it's because he's not worried about the threat. And the only reason a wolf doesn't worry about a threat, is if he plans on removing it."

I glanced down at Jesse. He was snoring softly.

"He's asleep," I told Rocco.

Rocco barked out a laugh. "Hunting wolves don't sleep."

I blinked. "At all?"

"They don't sleep at all," he repeated. "The magic and the pheromones keep him awake. After he's bitten you and met your wolf, he'll sleep for a whole damn week."

My eyebrows lifted. "I'm in over my head." I brushed hair out of my eyes. "How is this my life?"

"It's not all bad. Come to dinner tonight; you'll see." He paused. "No stripping this time, though."

I scoffed. "I wasn't actually making a move on you. I just wanted the wolf to flip out so I could escape. I do actually wear shirts most of the time."

"I know. Still, come fully-dressed."

My eyes narrowed. "Why did I make you uncomfortable, anyway? I'm sure you've been around plenty of naked women before."

Rocco laughed uncomfortably. "For some reason, werewolves are only ever born male. Female werewolves have to be made. We haven't spent much time around women our age."

"It's not like you're virgins," I interrupted.

There was a long stretch of silence.

"No freaking way," I leaned forward. "You're not."

"Wolves mate for life. Sex is part of mating. If we get anywhere near a naked woman who isn't our mate, our wolves take over."

That was a yes, to the virgin question.

A laugh sputtered out of me. I'd been assuming they were total tools, asshole player-types.

And they were *freaking virgins*.

I'd never been experienced compared to anyone around me, but compared to them, I was experienced.

"Well damn. No wonder you guys are so uncomfortable talking about mating," I remarked.

"I'm going to hang up now," Rocco said. "Text me if you decide to go on that date, so me and the guys can be ready to drag your changing body and a pissed-off Jesse out of the restaurant."

He hung up, leaving me chuckling as I stared down at the wolf. He opened his eyes, realizing that the charade was up.

"Virgins, huh?" I asked him.

He blinked, long and slow.

"It's kind of sweet. I always thought it was romantic to hear about the people who wait until marriage to have sex. I've regretted losing my virginity to Jimmy Cooper at the prom ever since it happened."

The wolf's ears flattened against his head, and a ferocious growl of the likes I'd never heard from him vibrated his chest and throat against my thigh.

Guess I shouldn't have said that.

"We broke up a few weeks afterward. You don't have to worry about him." I scratched the wolf's head. "If I go on a date, are you going to break our agreement and bite me?"

He bobbed his head once.

Dammit.

I huffed. "You could at least have found a way to tell me that. If I hadn't called Rocco, I wouldn't have known. Pissing you off and getting bitten don't seem like events that should logically coincide considering Rocco said biting me will mean you're giving yourself to me."

The wolf growled, but it wasn't an angry growl.

"I guess you did try to attack Kevin." I paused. "Twice."

Maybe even three times... I couldn't remember exactly how the fight had gone down.

He licked one of the scabbing scratches on my arm.

"Alright, I'll cancel. I don't think I want to have dinner with your friends, though," I warned.

He lifted his head and shoulders in what I could only think of as a wolfy version of a shrug.

I picked up my phone and reluctantly called Kevin. He answered on the third ring. "Hi, Teagan."

"Hey, Kevin. About tonight..." I bit my lip.

"You're canceling on me," he said. He didn't sound surprised, and I felt like shit for that.

"My ex-boyfriend and I just decided to get back together. It has nothing to do with you, I swear. I'm sorry to cancel like this," I apologized.

It was bullshit, of course. But he deserved an excuse that wouldn't make him feel like crap, regardless of whether or not it was the truth.

"Ah, I get it. Well, send me a text when you're single again."

"I will," I agreed, even though it was kind of dickish for him to just assume I'd be single again at some point. What if my pretend ex was the one for me?

We exchanged goodbyes and hung up the phone.

A yawn stretched my cheeks. "Maybe I should take a little nap before I start studying," I remarked to Jesse.

His head dipped slightly in a small nod.

I slid off of the counter and walked to the couch, then took my shoes off before collapsing on the big, comfortable thing.

Napping in a bed would've been nicer, but until I could afford new sheets or even just took the time to wash Jesse's sheets, I wasn't going anywhere near his bed.

I fell asleep almost as soon as I was horizontal.

A LOW, threatening growling sound woke me up.

I shook my head, looking around the room. It was dark, and I didn't know how long I'd been asleep.

I heard paws clicking on the floor and tried to spot Jesse. He was moving around, but I couldn't see him.

More threatening growls and snarls came from the wolf.

Was someone outside? Or was someone in the house?

Panic blossomed within me.

What the hell was going on?

Paws sounded on the floor again, and red eyes came into view. I nearly screamed at the sudden appearance of the damn creepy things, but I cut myself off.

Jesse stared at me for a moment before his head whipped toward the door.

I relaxed slightly.

Guess the threat he was worried about was outside.

After walking slowly over to the wolf, I crouched beside him. "Do I need to call your friends?" I whispered.

He growled deeper.

Guess not.

The wolf snarled, nudging me toward the ground. I knelt beside him, then shuffled over to the window. He snarled again—that time at me.

"Shh. I want to see," I told him.

He snapped his teeth at me.

"You're not going to bite me," I whisper-snapped back.

At least, not yet.

I lifted one of the blinds covering the window, just barely enough to see outside. The porch lights were on, and I could see the front yard pretty clearly.

I watched... and saw nothing.

A frown dragged my lips down. "I don't know what—"

Jesse snarled and sprinted to the other side of the house. I flew to my feet and followed him to the patio door.

My hands landed on the glass as Jesse snapped his teeth and continued snarling. Another red-eyed wolf peered back at us.

SIXTEEN

I SCREAMED AND SKIDDED BACKWARD, toward the stairs.

Through the glass door, I watched as a human body came running toward us, from off to the side of the wolf. It was a guy—his hands in the air, his body completely naked.

I breathed a sigh of relief when I recognized Elliot—Smiley.

"It's Ford," he yelled through the door. "The wolf is Ford." He pointed over his shoulder. "We shift at night a lot. Lock your doors and Jesse will calm down!"

I let out a shaky breath and nodded.

Ford had warned me to lock the doors at night... I guess that was why. I couldn't remember unlocking most of them, but knew one or two were open.

I checked the back door as Elliot ran off into the darkness again. That one was already locked.

Making my way around the townhouse, I locked every damn door. When the lock clicked on the garage door, the last one, and the only one that hadn't already been locked, Jesse relaxed instantly.

How the hell had he known the garage door wasn't locked?

And why did he care?

Sure, he wanted to protect me, but he had to have realized that the guys outside were his buddies. And it wasn't like they were attacking his house or anything.

"Werewolves are so weird," I mumbled, making my way back to the couch. I needed to study, but I really needed to sleep and heal too. My test the next day would be a rough one, but it wasn't for one of my hardest classes, so I hoped I'd do okay enough.

Too tired for my responsible side to win out, I curled back up on the couch and fell asleep in seconds.

THE NEXT FEW weeks passed by quickly, with me and Jesse falling into a pattern.

He growled at me for not eating on the way to school, and I ignored him in favor of saving money. I avoided attractive men or men who seemed attracted to me like they were the damn coronavirus, and he didn't attack anyone. We studied together, slept cuddled together, and even bathed together when he started to smell and I threatened to get him neutered if he didn't.

He really did start to feel like a pet wolf.

...A really possessive pet wolf.

Honestly, he was the perfect companion. I wasn't someone who required much social interaction to get by, and I got what I needed at school and then had a buddy to hang with at home.

After a month, I decided I was tired of sleeping on the couch.

I was going to move in. Since we couldn't be apart after I became a werewolf (which I'd decided unfortunately did have to happen, since I wasn't ready to die) I dragged a chair to the fridge and grabbed Jesse's envelope of cash.

"I'm only spending this money on the bare minimum furniture," I warned Jesse the wolf. He was used to me talking to him like he was a person, and to responding like he was a person.

He tilted his head at me, his version of a shrug. He didn't care what I did with Human Jesse's cash.

"Seriously. This is Jesse's money, not mine. But I need a bed, and I'm not sleeping in Jesse's," I continued. "Even if I wash the sheets, that'll feel like accepting this prisoner-bride thing we've got going on. And I am not a prisoner bride."

The wolf snorted.

He didn't understand.

"Bare minimum, I swear." I wagged a finger at him. "Come on. I bet this town has a thrift shop."

I looked up directions, and found out it did.

But... I'd need a truck.

I glanced over at Jesse's phone, sitting on the kitchen counter where it had been since I'd last used it to call Rocco with another wolf question the week before.

With a sigh, I walked over to it. Rocco was the easiest of the pack members to deal with, as far as I'd learned, though Ford was a close second. But I still hadn't gone over to eat dinner with them, despite their many invitations, so I didn't really know them.

Rocco answered on the first ring. "Jesse?"

"Nope, still Tea. The wolf and I have an agreement, remember?" My hip rested against the kitchen counter.

"No one actually thinks he's going to stick to that. It's not much of a hunt if you set the terms," he reminded me.

"Well, you're not him. Anyway, do you have a truck?"

There was a long pause.

"I'm going to take that as a yes," I said. "Can I borrow it, or can you take me to the thrift store over on..." I glanced down at the location on my phone. "Grape Street? Seriously? Who names a street 'Grape'?"

Rocco let out a long sigh. "I don't know about that."

"Come on. I'll bring you..." I glanced at my fridge. The freezer was still fairly full, but I was on careful rations that meant I often skipped meals, much to Wolf Jesse's anger. I was still surviving, though. "A happy wolf friend."

A happy wolf friend? Seriously? That was what I came up with?

Rocco barked out a laugh. "If I come, I'll have to bring one of the other guys with me."

"I know, because you're afraid of my sexy lips and boobs. I'm quite seductive," I drawled.

"Not afraid, per say..."

"Bring whoever you want. I'm just tired of sleeping on a couch, so I need to buy a bed."

Rocco made a noise of disagreement. "You can't buy a mattress from a secondhand store, Tea. That's disgusting."

"Says the guy who turns into a wolf and has probably eaten poor innocent squirrels," I shot back.

"That's different."

Squirrel eating: another thing to add to the list of cons to becoming a werewolf.

"Is it, though?" I countered.

"It is. I'll take you wherever you want to go, but I'm not hauling a thrift store bed back to Jesse's place for you. He'd skin me alive."

I sighed. "Fine. We'll stop at a mattress store too."

I'd seen new mattresses at some thrift stores before, so I was crossing my fingers that the one in Moon Ridge sold them too. If I was going to spend Jesse's money, I was going to spend as little of it as possible.

"Alright. I'll grab one of the other guys and meet you in front of your place in ten minutes."

Well, that was service at its best and fastest.

I hung up, glancing down at my outfit. Shorts and a three-quarter sleeve top... not too sexy. I didn't want to scare my ride off, so that would do.

Putting on my shoes, I opened the cash envelope and stared inside.

So much money.

I pulled out two hundred-dollar bills and then put the envelope back. Taking Jesse's cash made me feel like shit, but I didn't have another option since I wasn't going to share a bed with him after he shifted back to human form.

Grabbing my bag, I headed outside as Rocco pulled his truck up in front of Jesse's house. I opened the door for my wolf, then followed him up onto the bench-style back seat after I tugged the door open for him.

I buckled myself in, and then Jesse's head landed right on my thigh just like usual.

"Hey," Rocco turned to shoot me a grin. "It's been a minute."

"Or a month."

"You sure do like to argue," he remarked.

"It's one of my best qualities," I agreed. "Hopefully I'm skilled enough at it to keep your friend away when he's back in human form and horny as shit."

Both guys laughed. I couldn't remember the second guy's name, but he had longish blond hair and light skin, like Rocco. Their faces were totally different, so despite their similar coloring, I didn't think they were blood-related.

"Good luck with that. Jesse's sweet-talked his way out of two dozen speeding tickets since we were sixteen."

"Two dozen? How fast does he drive?" I shot an alarmed look at the wolf on my leg. He lifted his wolfy lips, flashing me a toothy grin. "And how old are you guys?"

"We're all twenty-two. Packs are put together based on when babies are born, so we've all got birthdays within three months," Rocco explained.

So twenty-four speeding tickets in six years? He was never driving me anywhere.

"What was your name again?" I asked the new guy.

"Dax." He nodded my way. "You should join us for dinner sometime. We'd all like to get to know you."

"And we're all missing Jesse," Rocco added.

"I'll try to send him over for dinner, then," I said, though I doubted I'd talk him into it. And I still wasn't sure I was ready for socializing with Jesse's kidnapping werewolf buds.

"He won't leave you," Dax warned me.

"Probably not," I agreed.

Rocco turned the radio on, so there was no awkward silence. My fingers stroked Jesse's ears. I'd gotten used to touching him; too used to it. I was going to go into withdrawal when I didn't have someone to cuddle with all the time.

And no, Jesse the man was not going to make my cuddle list. Currently, the only people on said list were Jesse the wolf, and my mom when she and I were both tipsy.

As far as my mom went, I'd told her that I adopted a dog and moved to a rental house. She thought I had a roommate to help me afford the place, and she thought I'd been promoted at the sandwich shop so I had the money.

I felt bad about lying to her, but I couldn't exactly tell her I was being hunted by a werewolf.

Rocco parked in front of the thrift store, and glanced back at me. "What are we looking for?"

"Hopefully, a cheap mattress, dresser, and desk. I've got two hundred bucks to spend, so if I can't find a cheap enough mattress, I'll just keep living out of my suitcases and buy the cheapest thing the mattress store has."

Both guys turned to look at me.

"You found Jesse's cash stash, right?" Dax looked concerned. "If money's a problem, we can—"

"I found his cash. I'm not going to spend it unless I don't have another option. Two hundred is plenty." My voice was firm.

Rocco's eyebrows knitted together. "He wants you to spend the money, Tea. That's why it's there. Giving our mates something makes us feel less shitty about ruining their lives."

"Well if he wants to feel less shitty about that, he'll have to find some other way to make it up to me." I reached for the door.

Rocco hit the button to lock it. "That's not gonna fly." He hit a button on his phone and lifted it to his ear. I frowned when there was a short pause, but then he spoke into the phone. "Hey, Mama Yates." Another pause. "No, Jesse's fine. Yep, he and Teagan are right here." He glanced at me.

Mama Yates? Obviously that wasn't Rocco's mom, but it couldn't be Jesse's...

Could it?

I looked at the wolf. His ears were perked up, listening.

"Do you still have Jesse's old mattress? Tea's apparently been sleeping on a couch, and she's not willing to spend Jesse's cash or sleep in his current bed."

Shit.

It *was* Jesse's mom.

Rocco chuckled. "Yep. We'll be right over. Thanks." He hung up and looked at me. "It's your lucky day. We found you a bed, and it's free."

"You are not taking me to Jesse's mother's house," I warned.

"Yes I am." He pulled out of the thrift store's parking lot and pulled back onto Grape Road.

SEVENTEEN

"TURN THE TRUCK AROUND," I unbuckled my seatbelt, grabbing the back of Ford's seat. "Turn the hell around or I swear I'll kiss you again."

Jesse shoved his furry self between me and Rocco, growling at Rocco.

I found it extremely humorous that he chose to growl at *Rocco* for my threat, but the moment was far too serious to laugh.

"You don't get to decide when I meet Human Jesse's parents." My voice raised as I spoke. "I don't even know him, and they're going to assume I'm his freakin' mail-order-bride."

"No one thinks you're a mail-order-bride, Tea," Rocco said, over the sound of Jesse still growling.

"They won't assume anything," Dax added. "They're realistic people. No one expects a girl to be in love with her mate during the hunt."

"If there's one thing I've learned in the last month, it's that there's no such thing as a realistic werewolf." I glared at both of them. Jesse had me trapped back down on the seat, and my damn hands were scratching his fur for absolutely no apparent reason.

"If you think that, you should meet the main alpha. He's about as unrealistic as they come," Rocco muttered.

"Don't change the subject. You're trying to force me to meet the parents of a man I've never met—and probably won't like."

"Why do you assume you won't like him?" Dax asked.

"Quit changing the subject," I snapped.

Mostly because I didn't have an answer.

I had made it a point not to move any of his stuff or go through any of his things, mostly staying downstairs for everything other than bathroom trips, but I'd still picked up on a few things. And to be honest, from what little exploration I'd done in Jesse's house, I'd already realized there was a good chance I *would* like him. Maybe not as much as he wanted me to, but at least as a friend.

"Jesse's a lovable guy. Even if you don't like him at first, you'll learn to. He'll worm his way into your heart," Rocco said.

"Like the wolf did," I muttered.

Wolf Jesse gave me a toothy grin and licked my face.

Rocco parked in the driveway of a little house, surrounded by other little houses in a structured neighborhood.

"Shouldn't you leave the driveway free?" I asked, trying to put off the inevitable.

"Papa Yates works until 5, so there's no need." Rocco shot me an amused grin. "Come on, Tea. I thought you were braver than this."

"It's not a matter of bravery." I unbuckled my seatbelt and slid out of the truck, leaving the door open long enough for Jesse to hop out too. He brushed up against my side, as he liked to do when I was upset.

I used to hate that it calmed me, but I'd come to accept it.

We headed up a pretty stone path leading to the Yates' front door, and my eyes skimmed over the front lawn. The grass was still green, but the leaves on the tree were on the dead side of orange. Fall had hit with a vengeance, and had it been any later in the day, I would've needed a sweater.

I stayed behind Rocco and Dax as they knocked on the door.

A middle-aged brunette with smile-lines answered almost immediately. "It's been ages," she chastised the men, surging toward them and engulfing them in a hug. "You're supposed to be bringing me updates," she scolded.

"Sorry. Tea doesn't call very often," Rocco said.

Throw the blame at me, why don't you?

"Oh please. You know as well as I do that if you wanted to know how she was, all you'd need to do is show up with cookies. No one turns down free cookies."

She had a point. Even I wouldn't turn away someone who wanted to give me cookies.

She pushed past the guys, her eyes lighting up when they landed on me.

I braced myself for a massive hug from a stranger.

It didn't come.

"It's so good to meet you, Teagan." Her voice was warm, her smile bright and genuine. "I hope my son isn't giving you too much trouble."

Rocco snorted. "*She's* the one giving *him* trouble."

I fought the urge to flip him off.

"Then she's doing it right." She flashed me another of her big smiles.

Maybe I liked Jesse's mom after all.

"Come on in. Unlike the boys, I have cookies." She winked at me.

Okay, I definitely liked Jesse's mom.

Following them in, I nudged Jesse. "Go lick your mom," I whispered. "She probably misses you."

He gave me the stink-eye.

"A wolf would never lick someone other than their mate. It's a method of kissing for them," Jesse's mom told me as we approached her small but clean kitchen. She pulled a plate of chocolate chip cookies from the microwave, and my mouth watered just at the smell of them.

It had been way too long since I had chocolate *anything*.

The woes of being broke.

"I didn't know that," I told her.

"Clearly these boys haven't been fulfilling their role in explaining our world to you." She shot them an annoyed look that rivaled my own.

They both reddened, embarrassed.

Okay, maybe Jesse's mom was my hero.

"Wolves also don't like to be touched by anyone other than their mate's human." She gestured to my hand, which had somehow found itself in Jesse's fur once again. "When they brush up against you the way he's doing, they're marking you with their scent so others know that you belong to them."

I glanced down at Jesse.

No wonder he brushed up against me so often.

Jesse had let a few other women touch him on campus, but usually he managed to avoid it. Maybe when he let them, it was because he didn't see an alternative other than leaving the area he knew I was.

"But it's also a way to show affection," Rocco added.

"Right. You'll notice him sticking closer to you when you're upset," she agreed.

"I have noticed that. Is it weird that he licks my legs a lot?" I checked.

Jesse's mom chuckled. "That just means he likes you. I imagine he's getting excited about what your wolf may look like now that you're warming up to him."

My cheeks heated. "I'm not really warming up to him. We just have an agreement." I withdrew my hands from his fur, crossing them over my chest.

"Of course. Here, have a cookie." She lifted the plate toward me. "Boys, you know where Jesse's old room is. Go ahead and take the mattress." She looked at me as they headed toward his old room. "Did you need a dresser and desk?"

I nodded, my face burning hotter. I hated asking for help.

"The rest of the furniture, too," she called after the guys.

"Make sure those boys carry that furniture up those stairs for you. I don't want you hurting yourself in an effort to be independent," she warned. "I've been there, and it's not fun."

I nodded again, feeling a bit targeted. Sure, I liked to be independent, but I'd never hurt myself in an attempt to do so.

Well, not on *purpose* anyway.

"Do you have Jesse's phone?" she asked me.

"Yeah, it's in the kitchen in his house."

"The house will be yours too, as soon as you're ready to put your name on it. Mates share everything. It makes things simpler that way, even if they choose not to be romantic in their human forms," she explained.

My eyebrows lifted. "Are there many who do that?"

"Not many, but some." She gave me a gentle smile. "As I'm sure you're realizing, there's a certain peace that comes with having a built-in companion, regardless of any romantic feelings that follow or don't follow the mate climax."

I nearly cringed at her mention of the upcoming sexathon with a man I'd never really met. According to everyone, I'd be damn ready for it when it arrived, but still... that was weird to think about.

"Don't worry about my son pressuring you into anything." She set a gentle hand on my shoulder. "I taught Jesse clearly and repeatedly that his mate would be her own person. He knows that his job will be to make the transition as easy for you as he possibly can. When the hunt is over and he's back in his human form, things will be simpler."

"Except I'll be stuck in some wolf's brain while she decides if Jesse will make a good mate," I countered.

She scoffed. "Those boys... I'm going to have their hides. Your wolf won't take control while she hunts, Tea. She'll watch through your eyes, and take over when she desires. All common sense will fly out the window as she tests him. When my wolf was hunting, she ran into a mountain lion's den just to see if her male would follow her."

"Shit. Really?"

"Really. Female werewolves are much more vicious than males, largely because the wolves within us didn't grow up seeing through the eyes of their humans the way the male wolves did. It's a bit of a disadvantage."

"Is it worth it?" I wondered.

"Does it matter if it's worth it? There's no way out after a wolf has his sights set on you."

"Still..." I grimaced.

"I would give up my human life a hundred times over for the love I have with Mark, so to me, it's very much worth it. But there are some who don't feel the same, so whether it is to you depends on what you make of it. Being a werewolf's mate comes with a price, but it also comes with a wolf and man who will love you for the rest of your life, regardless of what you want and who you become. To me, that's worth just about anything."

The guys came back in, grabbing cookies off the plate and swiftly ending our conversation.

Jesse's mom winked. "I'll put the rest of these in a bag for you."

EIGHTEEN

I WALKED out of there loaded with cookies, feeling more confused than ever... and also just a little, tiny bit hopeful.

Rocco and Dax hauled Jesse's old furniture up to the spare bedroom for me. I hadn't ever really gone inside it, but I needed to move the stuff over to Jesse's room now that I was taking it over.

I followed them back down the stairs after they'd set everything on the ground in the spare room for me.

"Thanks, guys." My hands landed in Jesse's fur, like they always seemed to.

"You can thank us by coming to dinner." Rocco gave me a tentative grin. "We'd like to get to know you."

I was feeling too thinky to leave the house—and needed to study when I was done rearranging my room. "How about tomorrow?" I asked.

"Deal." Rocco offered me a hand.

I stepped toward him and puckered my lips, teasing him by reaching for his face. Dax grabbed me around the waist, spinning me away from Rocco, and I burst out laughing.

"I'm just messing with you guys. I'm not actually going to kiss you."

Neither of them looked convinced.

They really didn't know me, or my sense of humor.

"See you tomorrow," Rocco said quickly, and then they ducked out.

I was still grinning broadly as I walked to the front door. Locking it up, I turned to find Jesse eyeing me suspiciously. "It was a joke," I told him.

He growled.

"Seriously, it was just a joke. My lips are lonely, but not *that* lonely."

Jesse jumped up on his back legs, plopped his front paws on my shoulders, and licked me right across the lips. I shoved him off, spitting and gagging.

"Blech, that's nasty. You can't go licking people's mouths, Jess. That's just foul." I noticed his wolfy grin and narrowed my eyes. "My lips will never be lonely enough for a wolf kiss, alright?"

He made a coughing sound that was suspiciously close to a laugh.

Asshole.

"You're lucky you're cute and furry. If you were a guy, I'd kick you in the balls."

He did his cough-laugh again.

I flipped him the bird, shaking my head as I climbed up to the second floor. As cute as Jesse's townhouse was, a girl could definitely get tired of stairs.

I stepped into the spare room, AKA, my new bedroom.

Where to begin...

There were only a few pieces of furniture to drag across the hall to Jesse's room, so I decided to start with those.

I rolled the desk chair over, followed by a little side-table that held what looked like one of those forty-dollar crapshoot printers that would survive anywhere from a day to ten years, depending entirely on your luck.

Leaving those, I headed back for the desk. Since I hadn't been in the spare room for more than a few seconds before, I hadn't noticed the laptop sitting closed and plugged in on the desk, or the stack of papers beside it.

"What have you been up to, Human Jesse?" I murmured, leaning over the table.

I leafed through the papers, my eyebrows lifting higher with every one I saw. There were printouts from five different classes: applied programming, computer architecture, embedded systems, computer security, and web backend development.

What the hell were those classes for?

Sure, I could guess he was going after some kind of computer degree—that much was obvious. But computer security, applied programming... what would you need those for?

I went back to Jesse's room and grabbed my laptop off the floor where I'd left it, setting it down next to Jesse's and pulling up my school's course catalog. It took me about twenty minutes of comparing courses—the names weren't exact matches for whatever his college was and mine—before I realized what he was getting a degree in.

Software engineering.

I stepped over to the mattress on the floor, and sat down on it. Shoving hair away from my face, I stared at the closed closet doors.

Software-freakin'-engineering.

Who the hell *was* this guy?

I'd thought he was a jock who slept around (okay, I'd *assumed* that) but he was not only a freakin' virgin, but a virgin getting a degree in *software engineering*.

One who stocked up cash for a chick he'd never met, just because he wanted to ease her transition into his world.

"I think I'm going full-on Stockholm Syndrome," I told wolf-Jesse.

He licked my arm twice.

I didn't even push him away or tell him not to.

Because…

What if Human Jesse was kind of perfect?

What if he was nice to talk to, not just look at?

What if he was actually, legitimately someone I would've been interested in even without the whole werewolf mess between us?

Up to that point, I'd assumed there wasn't a chance in hell I could ever have feelings for the guy inside the wolf I'd learned to tolerate.

But what if I liked him?

Liked him, liked him?

Holy shit, I couldn't fall in love with a werewolf, could I?

"Calm down, Tea," I muttered to myself. Looking at Jesse, I said, "Turn around. I don't want your human to see me losing my ever-loving mind over here."

He huffed a sigh, but turned his head so he was looking the other direction.

"He can't be a hot nerd," I whispered. "There aren't that many of them, remember? Like, less than half a percent of the population."

Okay, that was a statistic I made up on the spot, but a girl had to tell herself what a girl had to tell herself. Fake statistics be damned.

But... software engineer?

"I'm just going to open his computer and check what he was looking at before reaching any conclusions," I muttered. "I'll probably find, like, a shit-ton of porn. And a cheating website—yeah, he probably cheats on all his classes."

The wolf snorted.

I flipped him off again, opening Jesse's laptop.

Yeah, major privacy invasion, but so was abducting a chick and forcing her to live in your house. He could get the hell over it.

The screen turned on instantly. He'd left it plugged in and running, so he'd been planning on coming back to it.

And what did I find on the screen after typing in the password his friends had given me (twelve-twelve)?

Homework.

Halfway-completed homework.

I went through all twelve open tabs. Eleven were related to his classes—actual homework screens he was working on, how-to videos, and a couple programs I didn't know that had computer language on them.

The twelfth?

A guide to stocking a brand-new home. There was a little box open on that tab that said, "print successful," so I grabbed the stack of papers and leafed through them again.

I didn't find the home-stocking sheet, though.

Frowning, I searched the rest of the office, and still didn't find it.

I went into Jesse's room, and checked the printer—it wasn't there either.

Skidding down the stairs, I pulled open drawers until I found the junk drawer I'd avoided like the plague.

When I opened it up, I found the list right on top.

Maybe it wasn't a junk drawer after all.

It was a two-hundred-fifty item list. Most of the items were crossed out, including pain meds, tampons, sanitary napkins, and a razor.

Things I was positive Jesse the man didn't need.

Dropping the paper back on the counter, I took the stairs two at a time and dropped to my knees in the bathroom, flinging open the cupboards. I'd never dug around in them

—not wanting to get too cozy. My own tampon box sat on the floor next to the trash can.

My lips parted when I saw the inside of the cupboards.

A massive pack of pads.

Fruit-scented shower gel, shampoo, conditioner, and deodorant.

Boxes of various sizes and brands of tampons, stacked to fill the cupboard.

Jesse had been nesting... on freaking *steroids*.

But to do that, he'd been looking up ways to make his future mate feel at home. Researching what she would need —what I would need.

What I would *want*.

I dropped to my ass on the tile floor, staring blankly at the cabinet.

The wolf stood in the doorway, watching me with a tilted head.

"Jesse's not a bad guy at all," I said quietly. "Is he?"

The wolf shook his head for "no".

"And he's a nerd," I said.

The wolf tilted his head, confused.

"He studies a lot, and is really smart," I clarified.

The wolf's head bobbed again.

"I'm going to like him," I groaned.

The wolf grew still.

I eyed him suspiciously. I'd never seen him freeze like that.

"What are you doing?" My voice grew cautious.

The wolf gave a small growl and stepped toward me like he was a predator.

"No, no, no." I shook my head, scrambling backward until my back hit the toilet, then the wall. "You said I had until Christmas, and it's not even November yet. I have classes—and grades. And I don't want to die, dammit!"

The wolf took two more steps toward me, and then he lunged.

NINETEEN

I SCREAMED as sharp teeth sliced into my hip through my clothes. My scream cut off as the pain vanished, giving way to a tingling numbness that made my hip feel like it was growing and swelling—and then like I couldn't move it at all.

The wolf's teeth slid out of my skin, and his tongue lapped at my wound as he whined. I pushed at his face, yelling something—or at least, I thought I was yelling something.

My head started to feel fuzzy, and my body began to sway.

Jesse the wolf dove to my side, cushioning my head's fall with his back just before I landed on the bathroom tile.

My heart beat rapidly, but I felt nothing as the world spun.

Cracking sounds, howls, whines, grunts, and shouts sounded in the room, but I felt nothing.

The world just continued to spin.

My eyes finally closed.

When I awoke, I heard steady breathing beneath my head. I tried to move, but couldn't. My eyes opened and closed slowly—but I wasn't controlling them.

Panic rushed through me when my body began to move—to freakin' *move*—while I didn't consciously move it.

My gaze landed on furry paws, then on a ruggedly beautiful human man sprawled out beneath me, entirely naked.

Horror tore through me as I realized what had happened.

Jesse had bitten me.

I was a werewolf.

The person controlling my body—her body—our body?

It was a wolf. My wolf. The Wolf Teagan.

She lifted her head toward the ceiling, and let out a loud howl.

My ears rang as she sang. I couldn't read the emotions in her song, I couldn't understand what she was saying or why she was howling or whether she was happy or sad or thrilled she had conquered me by taking control of my body.

The front door opened only moments after her song began, and heavy footsteps pounded the stairs as the wolf's pack ran to greet her.

Her gaze flitted from man to man. They looked between her and Jesse.

Elliot kneeled in front of her, his hands outstretched. "Teagan."

She lifted her chin, not walking toward him.

He pulled something out of his pocket, and the air smelled different.

It smelled… delicious.

He lifted a baggie of bacon.

The wolf studied him.

"I bet you're hungry," he remarked.

Her stomach growled.

He opened his bag, and the smell intensified.

And holy shit, if that was what meat smelled like to a wolf, it was no wonder they killed live animals.

"We need to put Jessie in his bed," Elliot said.

The wolf growled.

Apparently, she knew who Jesse was. And felt strongly about him—either positively or negatively.

"I know you don't want him moved, but he'll be more comfortable in his bed. And you can sleep with him on there. It's very soft."

The wolf made a disdainful noise.

"I'll have some of the guys make you steak if you let us move him. Steak is even better than bacon." He waved the bag in front of her face, and she shuddered.

Holy hell, that smelled better than anything else on the whole freakin' planet.

He tossed a piece of bacon in front of her, and she dove for it.

The monster ate that shit in one swallow—didn't even chew.

The men all chuckled.

Her glare moved around the lot of them, and they quieted.

"This is Ford, our pack's beta." Elliot gestured to Ford, who stood beside him and to his left. "And this is Dax, our delta. You know you can trust a beta and delta to take care of your potential mate." He tossed another piece of bacon closer to his feet. She snapped it up instantly, but jumped back into the place she'd been standing.

My wolf glanced down at the gorgeous, naked man.

She was hesitant to leave him; probably because he was the reason she existed. Or maybe because she wanted to kill him. I wasn't sure, but I was guessing it was the former based on what everyone else had said.

"Back up, guys," Elliot said gently.

The guys all backed up, except Ford and Dax. Elliot backed up with the others.

My wolf looked suspiciously at Ford and Dax.

But when Elliot tossed another piece of bacon just outside the bathroom, she lunged forward and gulped it down.

He patted her on the head, and she snapped her teeth at him. He chuckled. "Feisty like your human, huh?"

She snarled.

"Yeah, I know I'm not your mate. Just wanted to welcome you to the pack. If you come with me, I won't touch you again."

She sniffed the air. I didn't know what she was looking for, but she seemed to find it.

She gave Ford a long look, then gave Dax the same. A low, threatening growl vibrated her chest.

"We'll be careful with him," Dax vowed.

She flashed the men her fangs.

Elliot threw another piece of bacon, and she stepped further into the hallway.

Dax and Ford moved slowly into the bathroom. I couldn't watch them go, since I was looking out of the wolf's eyes, but they came back with Jesse's snoring body a moment later.

My wolf abandoned the bacon, following the men into Jesse's bedroom. They set him down on his bed and tossed a blanket over him.

My wolf sniffed the blanket, and then snarled at it.

"You want him naked?" Ford asked with a raised eyebrow.

She growled at him.

He looked at Dax, who shrugged. "I don't know how a female wolf thinks."

Ford grabbed the blanket and lifted it to his nose, sniffing. He made a face.

"Tea hasn't been sleeping in the bed. It's stale." He tossed it to the ground.

"She told Rocco she's been sleeping on the couch," Dax offered.

"I'll grab the blanket," someone called from downstairs.

A few minutes later, Rocco came back with my blanket hanging over his shoulder. My wolf growled at him. "It's alright, Tea. I'm the coolest one in the pack. Your human kissed me once, and almost kissed me a second time too."

My wolf snorted.

His grin widened. "I felt the same way." He tossed the blanket over Jesse's lower-half.

My wolf sniffed it, and it smelled fine to me. Not that the other blanket had smelled bad; I hadn't smelled anything from it.

She plopped down on the bed, her side curled up against Jesse's, and narrowed her eyes at Elliot. He was standing in the doorway, watching the interaction.

"Here." Elliot crossed the room, tugging the rest of the bacon out of the bag. He fed it to her piece by piece, and she made happy noises while she inhaled the food.

When it was gone, she growled.

"Zed's already cooking up some steaks," he promised.

She tilted her head.

"He's our Sigma," Rocco told her.

She nodded, like that meant something. The only pack roles I'd heard about were alpha—which I knew Elliot was—and omega, which Jesse was.

"We know you won't leave your wolf form until Jesse wakes up, so two of us will be here at all times until then, alright?" Elliot checked.

My wolf huffed and lowered her head to her paws.

"I know you'd prefer to be alone with him, but he's vulnerable like this. And you are too."

She gave an irritated growl.

Elliot chuckled. "Omega through and through."

What the hell did that even mean?

"Jesse hates having to rely on people too." Elliot perched on the edge of the bed, beside my wolf. She sniffed at him, found him suitably non-threatening, then lowered her head back to her paws.

She seemed to take comfort in feeling Jesse's chest rise and fall against her side as he breathed. That, or she just didn't trust the pack.

I wouldn't blame her for either one.

The men continued chattering around her, but she was tired. While her steak cooked, she slept. I had no choice but to sleep when she did, my consciousness dependent on hers.

MY WOLF PLAYED house with the pack members for an entire week, and I started to pick up on the group's dynamic a bit more. I learned that as the sigma, Zed was the troublemaker, but he was wicked-smart. And that as the gamma, Rocco was the jokester, but he was also the one you could tell anything to. And as the alpha, Elliot was basically the papa bear. He always had snacks, and looked out for everyone while setting them all at ease.

They were on day nine of wolf-sitting when Jesse finally opened his eyes.

The first thing said eyes did when they opened?

Land on my wolf.

A sharp pain cut through my spine, and I screamed as the shift back to human form began.

TWENTY

"GET SOME PANTS FOR JESSE," someone yelled.

Another crack in my spine—another scream.

"Does Tylenol work on newly-changed humans?" another guy demanded.

Another snap—another scream.

"Of course not, moron!" a third guy yelled.

Another break—I was pretty sure I was crying at that point.

"All of you shut up," a new voice snarled. "She doesn't like to be crowded."

The voices went silent.

I just kept screaming.

More bones broke, more tendons snapped, and more terrible, horrible pain ensued.

When it finally stopped, I was panting and sweating. I was wrapped in something—a blanket? I didn't know, but I wanted it off my skin. I wanted to freakin' breathe, and feel my own damn body.

I fought the blanket.

"Everyone out," the new voice commanded.

The door closed less than a second later, and the blanket was ripped off of me unceremoniously. The yank on the blanket rolled me smack into a bare, chiseled chest connected to a pair of arms that had apparently been loosely wrapped around me and the smothering blanket.

I opened my eyes, looked into the new pair, and growled, "Get the hell away from me. I don't know you."

His hands left my body like I was on fire.

The door flew open.

"Rocco!" I yanked a blanket back over my chest even though the last thing I wanted was to wear anything. "Get me a towel and help me to the bathroom."

The blond had the audacity to look to Jesse, like he was looking for permission.

"I will rip your balls off," I snarled.

Rocco disappeared, and reappeared with a towel. He tossed it my way, and when I failed to catch it, Jesse did.

"Here." He handed it to me.

Standing on sore, shaky legs, I wrapped the thing around me and stood.

"Let me—" he began.

"I know you were inside the wolf, watching me, but I'm not comfortable with you touching me right now," I said sharply. "I don't know you, and I feel like I was just body-snatched by a damned alien."

He nodded slowly, lifting his hands out in front of him. "I get that. But you're going to fall over if someone doesn't help you, and I don't know how my wolf is going to react if any of the other guys touch you. He's very possessive."

My wolf hadn't left Jesse's freakin' side for nine days except when she needed to pee, so I got that. That was reasonable.

"I'll walk myself, then."

The other guys scattered when Jesse shot them a look. Their feet were loud on the stairs.

Even though it meant I was alone with Man Jesse, I was glad they were gone.

My toes felt weird, my legs awkward after so much time in a different form. I took two steps and then stumbled. Jesse reached for me, but I grabbed the doorframe instead.

"Tea..."

"I'm fine," I hissed, biting my cheek to ignore the discomfort.

"It gets easier. Your body adjusts," he said.

"I was there in the van when you shifted after we met. That was not easier," I said through clenched teeth.

"I was fighting my wolf, trying to give the guys time to get us away from a human-populated area. It's not usually that bad."

I scoffed. "Yeah, right."

"I'm serious. You'll learn to feel it when your wolf starts to take over, and if you give her control instead of fighting her, it'll be less painful. It just takes time to get there."

"Excuse me for not trusting you."

Jesse sighed. He ran a hand through his hair.

I pretended not to notice that it was a glorious chocolate color, and long enough that I could feel its silk on my skin if he—

Bad, Tea. Bad.

I felt what he said—the wolf pressing forward, trying to take control.

"Shit! It's happening!" I panicked, grabbing the doorway with both hands and holding tight. "Back the hell off, wolf! I just got my damn legs back!"

"Panicking isn't going to help. Come here," Jesse plucked one of my arms off the doorway and draped it over his shoulder. The physical contact immediately gave me goosebumps. "She doesn't want you to leave me, the same way my wolf didn't want to leave you. Show her that you're not walking away, and she'll stop. Probably."

"Probably?" I hissed.

"It's not an exact science; they're animals. Give me your other arm," he said, dragging it off the doorway. With a soft tug, he pulled me all the way into his arms and hugged me.

When he was holding me securely to his chest, my wolf began to retreat.

"I think she's stopping," I breathed.

"Mmhm," Jesse murmured. His nose was in my hair, his eyes shut as he held me.

"Are you sniffing me?" I started leaning away.

"Shh. Give her time." He gave my waist a gentle squeeze.

I found myself leaning my face against his chest. He was the perfect height; my head would fit right under his chin if he wanted it to.

Of course, right then he just wanted to sniff me. Like a damn weirdo.

"I think you just wanted to hug me," I mumbled into his bare chest.

"I won't deny that."

At least he was honest.

And did I mention how much I liked his bare chest? The muscles on that man... phew, a girl didn't see muscles like those very often. And if he was shallow, I wouldn't have been interested in said muscles, but knowing that he was majoring in software engineering and that he had an envelope of money saved for me and a cupboard full of tampons...

Well damn, if that didn't make me attracted to his muscles nothing would.

And as much as I hated to admit it, being in his arms started to relax me. My body began to settle, the wolf disappearing back into wherever the hell she was. My legs even started to feel a bit more normal.

"What are you doing to me?" I spoke into his chest again. That time, I noticed the flex of his muscles as his body reacted to my lips on his skin.

And well, I liked that reaction… a lot.

But I wasn't admitting that.

"It's part of mating. No one's told you shit," he said into my hair. "You scared them away when you kissed them all."

I snorted. "Most guys aren't *afraid* of kissing."

"We're not most guys."

"I've gathered that." I closed my eyes and inhaled again slowly. Something about the way he smelled just made me feel like everything was going to be okay. "Alright, you can let me go."

"Can I?" he teased.

I smacked him on the arm. "Let me go."

With a sigh, he released me. I immediately felt more on-edge than I had when I was in his arms, but I'd get right the hell over that. No way was I spending the rest of my life wrapped in Man-Jesse's arms, even if they were very nice arms.

"I'm going to take a shower to try to feel a little more human again," I told him. "Stay out here." I pointed outside the door, like I had when he was a wolf.

"Your wolf's not going to like that," he warned.

"You're not going to sit in here and watch me shower, no matter who you are." I started to close the door. He caught it, leaning his head toward me.

Dammit, why were his eyes pretty too?

Dark green, like the forest right after the sun disappeared... they were freaking gorgeous.

"If your wolf starts to take over, just shout," he told me. "I can sit there on the toilet seat while you shower, with the curtain closed, and she'll be a lot more manageable."

"I'll be fine." I closed the door, and he didn't stop me.

I immediately felt that awful feeling of the wolf about to take control. "Jesse," I called out in panic.

The door swung open.

I waited for his smug expression and words, but they didn't come.

He just stepped into the bathroom, shutting the door behind himself.

The feeling of my wolf trying to force her way out didn't go away, though.

"Can you do the thing, where..." I gestured between us.

His arms wrapped around me, and he held me to his chest. The wolf relaxed immediately.

"Dammit," I huffed.

"It'll get easier," he promised.

"Quit saying that. Let me live in my misery," I grumbled.

He chuckled. "You want to be miserable? Fine. You've got an uncontrollable animal inside you. There's no way to get rid of her, and the only person she responds pleasantly to is me, a guy you don't know. You went out to get yourself a bed so you wouldn't have to sleep in mine, but tonight you're going to realize that she won't let you sleep away from me, and one way or another we're either going to end up cuddled together in a bed or on the floor."

He continued, "You're also going to find yourself extremely hungry in the next few minutes, to the point where you could probably consume an entire ham on your own and still feel hungry. Your grocery bills are about to shoot through the roof. And sometime in the next few days, you'll have the extremely-pleasant experience of watching your wolf hunt and eat a small animal."

"I hate you," I groaned, smacking him in the chest.

"Hate's not that far from love," he remarked.

"Mention love again and I will let my wolf take over next time," I said into his pec.

"Vicious," he drawled.

"Very." I let go of him. "Alright, sit on the toilet like a heathen."

"Yes ma'am." He shot me a grin, plopping down on his ass on the closed toilet lid.

I'd never seen someone so happy to sit on a toilet. But I didn't want to hear the reasoning behind his grin, so I just turned on the shower.

TWENTY-ONE

STEPPING in at the back of the shower, I tugged the curtain into place before I tossed my towel over it so I didn't flash Jesse as I stripped. When I slid under the water, I breathed a sigh of relief as the sweat of the last nine days began to wash away.

I heard a noise and peeked out the curtain, expecting to see Jesse staring at the outline of me or something. Instead, I saw him slouched against the wall. My towel was bundled up under his head like a pillow, and wrapped around his neck like a scarf.

A snore escaped him, and I bit back a grin before closing the curtain.

I'd never been really close to a guy before. I'd definitely never seen one fall asleep, and on a toilet, no less. I'd had three boyfriends, but none of the relationships had ever gotten serious. I'd only even slept with the one guy—Jimmy Cooper. That was a mistake, but you live and you learn.

I took my time in the shower, but as I rinsed shampoo from my hair, I started to get hungry.

Really hungry.

My stomach growled loud enough to rattle the damn townhouse, and Jesse's snores cut off abruptly.

"Tea?" His voice was groggy.

It was hard to remember that even though he seemed new, he'd been following me around for more than a month. So I didn't know him, but he knew me.

"Yeah, I'm fine," I called back.

My stomach growled again, and I nearly groaned.

Holy shit, was my body eating itself?

I slapped conditioner on my hair and washed it out without waiting for it to work its magic, then shut off the water. Slipping my hand out of the shower, I reached for the towel rack. It usually had a couple of towels on it, but Jesse's friends had been taking turns staying with us, and they didn't restock things the way I did.

"Here." Jesse put the towel in my hand.

I left my hand there, cringing. "Did one of your friends use this towel?"

Jesse took it back and sniffed it. "Nope. All I smell is you."

Phew.

I accepted the towel and wrapped it around myself before drawing the curtain back.

Jesse's eyes trailed down my body, and I put a hand on my hip. "You're not seriously going to check me out while I'm standing right here, watching."

His throat bobbed. "Sorry. It's natural. You're gorgeous, and you're my mate. I'll try to keep it under wraps."

Well, I didn't mind the compliment.

Shaking my head, I strode toward the bedroom I'd claimed. Jesse followed me there, which was only slightly annoying.

"Can you wait outside?" I asked him.

"I can, but I'm not sure you'll be alive to let me in afterward, the way your stomach's growling."

My lips twitched, threatening to lift upward in a grin. "Fine. Just close the door, and turn around."

He did as instructed, and I dressed quickly before wrapping my hair in the towel. It was going to stay up like that for a bit so it didn't drip everywhere while I ate.

"When we go down there, it would be good if you tried not to touch the other guys," Jesse said as we headed toward the stairs. "My wolf's kind of..." he ran his fingers lightly over his collarbone, and it took major effort for me not to stare at him in fascination as he did.

I forced my attention away from his bare chest and collarbone. "Kind of what?"

"Testy."

I got the feeling that wasn't the word he'd wanted to use.

"And by testy, you mean possessive?"

"Yeah, but you're not a fan of that trait."

"No, but watering it down doesn't make me more fond of it. I get it; I saw how your wolf reacted to everything. I'll keep my hands to myself this time."

He looked relieved. "Thanks."

"Thanks for the...that." I gestured to the bathroom as we passed it.

"The hugs?"

"Yep."

Wow, I was awkward.

"You don't have to thank me. I like hugging you, and it calms my wolf too."

Awkward. He made it more awkward.

Luckily, we reached the bottom of the stairs.

"There's our new she-wolf," Rocco grinned, holding his arms out.

Jesse swore and went stiff.

"Now you want to hug me?" I lifted an eyebrow. "Where was this Rocco when I actually *wanted* him?"

Rocco's grin widened. "You never wanted me. You just like making me squirm."

I laughed; it was true.

Jesse swore again, and I bit my lip.

Was I supposed to just... touch him?

Wouldn't that be weird?

His face was getting paler by the second, so I just went for it. I ducked under his arm, pulling it over my shoulder so our sides met, and I wrapped my arm around his waist.

He instantly relaxed and regained color. "Thanks," he murmured.

"Aw, how cute. Our first mated pair," Ford smirked our way.

My wolf threatened to take over, and I staggered a bit.

Shit.

"Not mated," Jesse said quickly. "Her wolf hasn't chased me yet."

That calmed her right down, for whatever reason.

"Let's talk about something that isn't the two of them," Elliot suggested, gearing the conversation in another direction. "Tea, you'll be happy to know that we hacked into your email account and let your professors know that you were attacked by a dog and hospitalized. The Moon Ridge doctor was happy to send a note to excuse you. Your professors have been sending heaps of homework your way, but your scholarship is intact."

I stood straighter. "Seriously? Thank you guys. That really means a lot."

"It was Jesse's idea. He made Ford and Dax agree to it when they dropped him in bed, before he crashed." Zed gestured over his shoulder, from where he was cooking steaks again.

I looked at Jesse, surprised he'd thought about me when he was so out of it. "Thanks."

He bobbed his head and led me to the table. We sat down beside each other, ready for the next inner-wolf attack.

The guys talked and joked. They brought me and Jesse into the conversation a couple times, but we were both a little out of it.

My stomach growled louder than the guys talking, and everyone laughed. The steak wasn't ready yet though, so I dropped my head to the table and shut my eyes.

I could go for a nap.

But... there was so much studying to catch up on.

I was going to need an entire gas station's worth of energy drinks to get caught up.

Jesse got up and walked to the fridge. He grabbed a plate, and then loaded it up with leftovers from what the other guys had been eating over the week. When he came back with it, he set it in front of me.

I lifted an eyebrow at him.

"You need to eat. You rarely even eat two meals, so I know you don't have the muscle or fat stores to power a werewolf's body. The way you're fueling yourself isn't enough anymore," he said.

I wanted to throw the plate at him, but he was probably right.

Picking up the fork, I got to work.

I was nearly done with the plate when the other guys brought over a thick steak with mashed potatoes and veggies.

I inhaled all of that one, next.

Jesse brought me seconds.

It freaked me out, but somehow I managed to eat all of that too.

I was halfway through my third plate before I managed to feel even somewhat satisfied, so I finished the third.

Ford whistled at me. "Usually Rocco pounds the most food. I'm thinking we're going to have a new champion soon."

My face flushed.

I didn't know why, but that was insanely embarrassing.

Jesse grinned. "Only until she's adjusted to being one of us. Then Rocco will have his trophy back." It was the first time I remembered seeing him really grinning, and he looked damn good doing it.

His expression and words deflated my embarrassment.

Then his knee bumped mine under the table, and the contact deflated it even more.

I shot him a grateful look, and he winked.

He actually *winked*.

Somehow, I'd ended up magically paired with a winking, gorgeous nerd who lived a secret life as a werewolf.

That definitely hadn't been in my ten-year-plan, but I wasn't quite sure complaining was the right thing to do, given that he was a hot nerd who'd just casually fixed the awkwardness in a conversation and then *winked* at me.

The werewolf thing though... yeah, I still wasn't sure about that.

Since Jesse and I were both awake and alive, the other guys decided they were going to head out.

They all stayed to help clean up, and then took off one by one. Elliot was the last to leave, and reminded me again that I could call or stop by with any questions I had at any time.

When the door closed behind him, me and Jesse were alone.

TWENTY-TWO

I LOOKED AT HIM.

He looked at me.

The house was clean for the most part, but I had a shitload of studying to do... and I still wasn't really feeling like myself.

I bit my lip. "I've got to study." Making up all my missed schoolwork was going to be a nightmare. "Want to go to the gas station to buy an energy drink with me?"

I only asked because I doubted I'd be able to walk away from him without the wolf in me taking charge.

There was disapproval in his stare. "Those are terrible for you."

"Well, they're great for my grades."

Honestly, they were more expensive than I could afford, but I couldn't afford not to drink caffeine either. It would affect me too much.

Jesse strode to the kitchen. "How about I just make you a pot of coffee?"

I made a face. "I've never gotten into drinking that stuff."

"Come here." He gestured me toward him.

I lifted an eyebrow.

"Come on. Unlike my wolf, I don't bite."

My fingers went to my hip.

I hadn't even thought about looking at the scar there—even when I was in the shower. Damn, I was out of it.

"I will carry you if I have to," he warned.

I shot him a dirty look and made my way over. With a dramatic sigh, I slipped up onto the counter.

"Let's make a deal," he said.

"I have absolutely no reason to make a deal with you. You're the reason I'm here, struggling to maintain my GPA." I gestured in a circle to the house around us. "Instead of in my dorm room, consuming information and loving every minute of it."

"That's true," he agreed. "But now you're stuck with me, so you may as well hear me out and consider it."

He wasn't wrong.

I gave him a long sigh. "Fine."

"I'll make you a cup of coffee—the best cup of coffee you've ever had. Assuming you like it, I'll agree to make as much coffee for you as you want, for the rest of your life, if you agree to never consume an energy drink again."

I scoffed. "That's a terrible deal both for you and for me."

"Alright." He amended the deal. "Assuming you like the coffee, you agree to only drink energy drinks in an emergency, twice a month at most. And I make you up to three cups of coffee a day, on the house."

Well, that was slightly more realistic.

"Why do you care?" I checked.

"Our lives are tied together now. What affects you will affect me. I've done a lot of research and don't like the way energy drinks work on our bodies, so I don't want you to have any adverse health benefits from them—however unlikely those are."

I rolled my eyes. "You're a health freak."

"No, I just prefer natural foods. Coffee is natural, therefore, it's healthier. Even if it is loaded with sugar and milk." He gestured to the French press on the kitchen counter. It hadn't been touched since I'd been living there.

"Fine. *If* I like it, I'll *consider* agreeing to your deal. There will be no swearing off energy drinks today, though."

"I can work with that." He grinned.

I studied him as he grabbed ingredients like he'd done it a thousand times. He probably had. It was pretty simple; he pulled some creamer from the fridge that I hadn't touched, sniffed it, and set it on the counter. Next came the sugar, and coffee grinds. The smell was pleasant enough as he prepared it.

There was a tightness in his shoulders that surprised me, and a pride that made me think he was a sly bastard for talking me into our little agreement.

Jesse's charm wasn't exactly what I'd been thinking when Dax and Rocco told me he'd talked his way out of two-dozen tickets, but I was starting to understand what they meant. He wasn't *charming* so much as *stubborn*.

Kind of like… me.

"So about tomorrow," Jesse said as he stirred the contents of the French press.

"What about it?" I grew suspicious again.

"It's Friday. Are you going to your classes?"

My suspicion deepened. "Are you going to ask me to stay home and grow wolf babies for you?"

He barked out a laugh, looking back at me with a grin. "Yeah, right. I don't want kids yet. Do you want kids yet?"

"*Hell* no."

"That's what I thought." He turned back around. "I was going to ask if you want me to go to your campus with you, since you probably won't be able to go without me. We can come up with an excuse as to why I need to stay with you, if you want."

My suspicion was replaced by surprise. "You'd do that for me?"

"Of course."

"You say that like it's a given, but it's definitely not."

"It is for me." He put his spoon down on the counter and turned to face me, remaining where he was. "I want to make this easier for you, Tea. I know it's a pain, in a lot of ways. I know I screwed up your plans and this isn't what you saw for your future. But I'm here, now, and I'm going to do what I can to make it as simple as possible for you."

Wow.

Okay, then.

That was actually really sweet.

"Most of my professors wouldn't notice or care if there was an extra student sitting in on their lectures. One of them would, but maybe if I show him my hip, he'll be lenient. We can say you're my brother or something."

Jesse lifted an eyebrow at that, and my face flushed.

"Fiancé, then. There's no way they're going to let you stay if you're just a boyfriend."

He nodded. "I can play along."

"I'm sure it'll be a real hassle," I said dryly.

He grinned. "A real hassle. Touching you, kissing you, holding you... I don't know how I'll survive."

I rolled my eyes, and his grin widened before he turned around.

His hands moved quickly as he assembled the drink, and then he put a warm cup in my hands. "Drink it now, while it's the perfect temperature."

I obliged. Lifting it to my lips, I took a tiny taste.

Bitterness melded with sweet. There was a lot of creamer in it, which definitely helped with the flavor. It wasn't the worst thing I'd ever tasted.

But I still didn't like it.

I glanced at Jesse's hopeful expression. I wasn't usually a sucker, but I didn't want to crush his dreams. "It's good," I sort of lied. "Not as good as energy drinks, but good."

His grin widened. "You'll think about giving up Red Bull?"

"I'll think about it," I agreed.

No way in hell was I going to swear away my Red Bull rights, but maybe I could get used to drinking coffee sometimes. It would save some money, and I wouldn't have to ration my caffeine so much since Jesse was so keen on making it for me.

I chugged the coffee before we headed upstairs. The caffeine would kick in faster that way, and I needed it badly.

Heading back to my new room, I ignored Jesse's lingering presence in the doorway as I put his papers in the desk drawer before I started dragging it toward his room.

"Easy." He grabbed the dresser from me, picking the thing up like it wasn't a legitimate piece of furniture.

I tried not to drool over the way his muscles looked all flexed like that, and only half-succeeded.

"What are we doing with this?" he checked.

"Putting it in your room," I gestured to the hall.

He gave me a chastising look. "I told you, your wolf's not going to let us sleep apart."

"And I told you I'm not sleeping in your bed." I shot him the same look back. "Regardless of the wolf that's trying to swallow me whole, I'm a human. I still don't really know you. And I'm going to do human things, like having my own room. You and I are roommates, not bedmates."

Jesse didn't seem put out by that. "I agree. I'd like to take things slow, too. But I'm telling you, your wolf won't sleep away from me."

"And I'm telling you I'll deal with that problem when it gets here. *If* it gets here. For now, we're going to put your stuff in your room and my stuff in my room. Got it?"

He looked... amused.

Hell, maybe even happy.

What was wrong with this guy?

"Yes ma'am." He saluted me.

I gave him the middle-finger salute back, and he busted up laughing.

"What is so funny?" I asked, getting exasperated.

"I'm sorry. It's just, werewolves grow up hearing about how you'll meet your mate and she'll be beautiful and perfect and everything. But that all sounds kind of dry. I thought it would be this whole dramatic ordeal, but we're standing here, and you're telling me off, and it's just... fun. I'm really damn glad it's you." He gave me a big, genuine grin.

Yeah, he was definitely insane.

But also, kind of cute.

"Alright, well, I'm not sure what to say to that. So take that desk in there." I shooed him toward his bedroom.

With another grin, he carried it easily across the hall.

I began moving my new-to-me mattress into the corner of the room to make space for the desk. When that was done, I started dragging my desk. That sucker was freakin' heavy.

Jesse came back in, plucking it up off the ground and looking to me for instructions.

I pointed where I wanted it to go, and he set it there while I grabbed the chair.

He moved the dresser after that, and then strode over to my suitcases while I grabbed my laptop and migrated to the desk.

I heard drawers opening and closing, and looked over to find him putting my clothes away.

"What are you doing?" I asked.

He glanced over. "Moving you in. You said you're claiming this room, right?"

"Yeah, but I can do that myself."

He shot me a knowing grin. "Let's be real, Tea. You're never going to make time for that. I've got time, so I'm doing it."

I opened my mouth to argue, but closed it when I realized he was right. I would never make time to put away my clothes when they were perfectly fine in piles in my suitcases.

"Fine. Leave the underwear." I looked back at my computer, pulling up the list of crap to do for my first class.

I groaned inwardly when I saw the list, and rubbed my eyes even though I could feel the caffeine kicking in already. That coffee packed a punch.

The next few days of catch-up were going to be hellish.

Jesse finished putting my clothes away—including my underwear, that bastard—and zipped up my suitcases, disappearing with them. He returned a couple minutes later with sheets, a comforter, and a book. After he made the bed, he dropped onto the mattress and made himself comfortable.

I glanced over at him and his book, and then did a double-take.

Eragon?

Talk about a classic.

And not one of those long, dry classics you read in English literature, but a classic that teaches you to actually enjoy disappearing into a fictional world.

"I'm so jealous you get to read fiction right now," I told him.

He chuckled. "You're the only thing on my to-do list until we're mated, so I exist only to read and make you feel good."

He paused.

To-do list? Ha.

I snorted, and his expression went sheepish.

He scratched his head. "I didn't mean that the way it came out."

"Well it's true, isn't it?" I shot back, wanting to see him blush.

His face reddened, and I mentally patted myself on the back.

"It's adorable that you're a virgin," I told him, flashing him a grin. "And so easily embarrassed." I shook my head, clucking my tongue. "Just thinking about how red your face is going to be when you're hit with the 'mate climax' hormones is enough to make me laugh."

"There won't be enough blood left in my face for me to blush. It'll all be in my—"

We looked over at his phone as it started ringing. He looked at the caller ID and grimaced, looking back at me. "It's the main alpha, checking to make sure you're alive. You okay if I take this in the other room?"

I shrugged. "Sure." It was nice that he'd asked, though. Usually guys would just cut me off and disappear.

He stepped out, and my chest sort of tightened as my wolf came to the surface, but with Jesse's scent all over the room and his voice floating in from the hallway, she remained calm for two minutes he was gone.

When he came back, my wolf settled and I dove back into anatomy memorization while he plopped back down on the bed and opened his book.

That was only the start of a very long night.

TWENTY-THREE

JESSE FELL ASLEEP AROUND two AM. He snored on my bed, snuggled up with his book, and it was kind of adorable.

Kind of.

I was too jealous of him to find it *completely* adorable.

Thanks to the second cup of coffee he made me twenty minutes before he crashed, I managed to stay up all night, and made a dent in the load of makeup work.

I nudged him awake ten minutes before it was time to go. He disappeared into the bathroom for a one-minute shower and came back smelling like river rocks and manliness that I probably shouldn't have been attracted to, but was.

He disappeared down the stairs while I finished shoving my stuff into my backpack. The wolf in me threatened to surface with his absence, but I was so tired that she too seemed sluggish.

When I landed at the bottom of the stairs, Jesse was waiting with two travel cups of coffee and a set of keys.

He handed me the coffee, and his hand met my lower back as he guided me out the garage door and into his car.

It wasn't until he was pulling out of the driveway that I remembered his friends' story about the tickets.

"Wait!" I yelled.

He slammed on the brakes, nearly killing us both in the process. "What? Who?" His head jerked side to side as he searched for a reason for my shout.

"You're a terrible driver. Swap seats with me." I reached down to unbuckle my seatbelt.

Jesse's hand blocked me, but he cracked a grin. "I'm a great driver. My friends just prefer to live on the slow side of things." He let go of my seatbelt and turned the wheel, pulling away from the house and heading down the road.

"I can't afford to get pulled over and miss this class," I warned Jesse.

"Then I won't get pulled over." The bastard winked at me.

I was starting to wish I could get the wolf back, though the human came with plenty of perks.

The way he looked was at least half of those perks. Maybe more.

SURPRISINGLY ENOUGH, I wasn't terrified while he drove. He didn't go too much over the speed limit, and never took a turn too sharp or anything. I assumed he'd taken my worry into account, and I appreciated it.

I finished my coffee halfway through the drive. When Jesse noticed me starting to fall asleep, he handed me his. I tried to protest, but he claimed he didn't want anymore.

Since I was pretty sure I'd crash without the extra caffeine, I drained the remaining half of his too.

He parked in the same place I always did. When I reached for my wallet, he shot me a dirty look and then paid while I got out and tugged my backpack over my shoulders.

"I'm not going to let you pay for everything," I told Jesse as we started walking.

"I know exactly how many dollars you have left to your name, Tea. Soon you're not going to have a choice." He strolled beside me, his body at ease. He wore a backpack too, but I wasn't sure what he'd put inside it.

"Over my dead body," I growled.

"You already defied death once. I doubt you'll have to tempt it again in the near future." The calmness of his words and his level of chill was frustrating.

A few people glanced our way as we walked past them. I felt my wolf threatening to take control, and my shoulders tensed.

"You know the money in that envelope is yours," Jesse reminded me, distracting me from my wolf.

"I know it's *yours*."

A beautiful brunette stared at Jesse way too long as she walked the opposite direction from where we were going, and I nearly fell on my face as a wave of pain sliced through my spine.

Jesse caught me, practically carrying me to the side of the walkway without letting anyone else see that he was holding nearly all of my weight. The pain vanished when his hands were on my skin.

"What the hell?" I hissed.

"What pissed your wolf off?" he murmured.

"I don't know." I spoke through clenched teeth. "Some girl was staring at you."

He gave me a sympathetic look. "Yeah, she's going to be possessive while she chases me. It'll help if we're touching."

I scoffed. "I hate this werewolf crap."

"I know." He helped me back to my feet. "Here," his hand slid down my arm, stopping when he linked his fingers with mine. The contact felt like... the most natural thing in the world.

My body was at peace, my fingers warm. As cheesy as it was, our hands fit perfectly together.

"See, this isn't so bad," he remarked, as we started walking.

Not so bad?

It was a hell of a lot better than 'not so bad'.

"Plus, anyone who looks at us will know we're together," he added. "That should help our inner-monsters."

Someone shot us a weird look, but I ignored them. It wasn't like I'd ever see them again, anyway. And crazy shit happened at college all the time.

JESSE and I ended up holding hands for most of the day. Every time we let go, my damn wolf would shoot the worst pain through my spine as she began to take control. It was miserable.

Not the hand-holding, but the wolf.

The hand-holding was... odd.

Oddly nice.

I didn't want to like it so much, but I did.

We headed home right after my last class. Jesse was as cheerful as he'd been all day, not seeming to mind one bit that he'd spent hours upon hours sitting in on lectures about stuff that had nothing to do with his degree.

While I spent the day trying to listen to the lectures rather than focus on how freaking good his hand felt in mine, he read articles about stuff that went right over my head and built some kind of 3D model on some engineering program he was apparently a wizard at.

I'd thought he was a dumb jock when we met, but clearly, I was very wrong.

And what was his backpack stuffed full of?

His laptop, and snacks. Like he was a mom with kids, in a grocery store. He seemed to have a sixth sense for knowing when I was getting hungry, which was often, and would hand me a granola bar or a bag of nuts or something before my stomach could even growl.

I can't lie; it was nice.

Not as nice as the way it felt when he held my hand, though.

Letting go of him when we reached the car was almost physically painful.

"You've got three tests to get through tonight?" he checked, as he pulled the car away from the school.

I nodded. "Yeah. They're all proctored online, so you'll have to be quiet."

He made a motion like he was zipping his lips. "Would you be up for pack dinner between exams?"

I hesitated. I'd sort of been avoiding his friends since the whole abduction and kissing situation; they were his friends, not mine. And clearly, they only liked having me around because their werewolf buddy decided I was his mate.

I wasn't really into that friends-through-someone-else thing. Either we were friends, or we weren't. And Jesse's packmates weren't my friends.

But... he'd spent the day following me around, feeding me. So I kind of owed him.

"You went to school with me, so I can do dinner with your buddies."

He shot me a look I couldn't read. "We don't have to. It was just a question."

"Yeah, but I'm sure you miss your friends. You've been stuck in wolf form for a long time, and—"

"And they're not friends, they're family. They get it. I do too. If you don't want to do dinner with them, we won't." He paused. "But they're nosy bastards. I give it three days, tops, until they start pushing to see us more."

I lifted an eyebrow in his direction. "They left me alone for way more than three days."

"That was before you were a female wolf," he said simply. "And before you wore my wolf's marking."

Shit... I still hadn't looked at that.

I tugged my shirt upward, exposing my hip where he'd bitten me. I wasn't sure if there was like, a typical place for a bite or anything, but it looked pretty gnarly. Though it was healed, the skin was a deep red color that clearly marked it as a scar from a bad injury.

"It's freaking huge." I shot Jesse a glare. The scar was twice as big as my hand, even with my fingers spread apart.

"My dick? Yes, yes it is."

Even surprised and pissed about the scar, I snorted at the joke. "The bite, moron."

"I didn't tell the wolf to make it that large, if that's what you're getting at. I can't communicate with him. If I could, I would've told him that breaking his promise to a lady was a damn good way to lose her trust."

"Is this normal though?"

He shrugged. "Every wolf marks their mate in a unique way. Some prefer small markings in hidden places, others prefer large scars in visible locations. Your mark is larger than most, but it's also fairly well-hidden."

"Well-hidden? I can't wear most of my clothes without flashing at least a little of this, Jesse." I gestured to my hip.

How had I not noticed the size of the thing? So much homework, so much coffee... dammit, it had distracted me.

"It's not on your arm or face," he pointed out.

"I will rip your *freaking huge* dick off your body if you don't quit arguing with me."

He shot me an amused grin. "Hey, Teapot. Quit calling this poor kettle black."

"Most teapots are not black, Kettle. That's not the saying. And—" I cut myself off, realizing I'd only confirmed his joke. "Dammit."

TWENTY-FOUR

WHEN WE GOT HOME, I set up my computer at the kitchen table so Jesse could cook. He volunteered, so I wasn't shooting him down. I felt a bit bad about turning down his request to eat with his buddies, so I vowed to myself that we'd go the next night.

I powered through the first exam while Jesse cooked. All three were due at midnight, which didn't give me a lot of time.

We ate between tests, and then I jumped into the second one. Jesse grabbed his computer and sat next to me. Not close enough for the proctor program to pick him up on the camera, but close enough that our legs brushed every time one of us moved.

I *may* have moved more than I needed to.

When the third test was done, I rubbed my eyes. Jesse set another massive plate of food in front of me.

"You're trying to fatten me up," I accused, though my stomach was growling silently.

He lifted an eyebrow. "You're a werewolf, Tea. That's not genetically possible any more. As you eat more, your muscles will fill out and your body will change a bit. But a werewolf can't eat too much."

I blinked at him.

Well, that was... nice.

Assuming I could eventually afford the grocery bills.

Until then, it would only be a disadvantage.

"I know that brain of yours is stressing about money. Don't. I've got it covered." He got up, headed to the bathroom while he left me with my food.

I expected my wolf's uncomfortable presence as he walked out of sight, but I didn't expect her to rip control out from under me like a damn rug.

A scream slipped through my lips as my back bent awkwardly, my bones starting to change and reform.

Jesse was back to me in a heartbeat, his arms wrapping around me while he whispered soothing words, but it was too late—the wolf was in control.

Agony bloomed, and withered, and then exploded repeatedly as the pain swelled and retreated again and again.

When the pain finally stopped, I was looking out through the eyes of my wolf.

"It'll get faster," Jesse promised.

I didn't know if he was promising that to me, or to the wolf who'd snatched my body. Either way, I wasn't looking forward to discovering that for myself.

He scratched my wolf's head, and she leaned in to his touch. Her eyes squinted slightly, and I wondered if she was analyzing him or something.

"Your human still has a lot of school work to catch up on, so if you're going to test me, let's get to it," he murmured at her.

She snuggled closer to him, licking his face, before she pushed out of his arms and moved to the back door. He stood, and gave her a stern look.

"Your food." He pointed to the plate.

The wolf huffed, but walked back to the food.

She swallowed it down in a couple of impressively large bites.

Had she even tasted it?

I was going with no.

She moved back to the door, and Jesse pulled it open for her.

Without a glance backward, she took off into the forest.

Clearly, she was not a pro when it came to logical thinking. Why the hell was she running *away* from our only tether to the werewolf world?

She was running like something was out to get her. Trees and branches and rocks flew past us as she sprinted her wolfy heart out.

I itched to take control, but I hadn't figured out how to do that; how to fight her.

Leaving her in charge of my body felt like a self-betrayal, but there was no alternative that I could see.

She must've run for an hour without a sign of anything but dirt and trees and other normal forest shit, but when she heard a soft rustle off to her side, she finally slowed. How she heard it was beyond me—I wouldn't have heard that tiny noise.

But she did, and stopped.

Her gaze narrowed in the direction the rustling had come from.

After all the animated movies I'd watched growing up, I half expected a bunny to jump out so we could laugh it off or something.

Instead, Jesse the wolf slipped out of the brush, his tail wagging.

He trotted up to my wolf and nuzzled her neck. She lifted her chin, letting him sniff her neck, followed by her sides and butt.

Wolves were so weird.

He was still sniffing when she must've decided she was done standing there, so she turned around and sprinted back into the forest without a glance backward.

Wolf Jesse caught up to her quickly, running at her side. They dodged branches and shit together. It seemed like hours had passed when they finally reached the row of townhouses that marked our home.

The wolves stopped in the forest and nuzzled each other a few times. I wasn't sure what they were doing, until pain spasmed in my spine.

Right.

Shifting back.

Yay.

I cried out silently, agony tearing through my body again as it began to change.

When the pain was finally gone, I was face down in the dirt, bare-assed and utterly exhausted. One of my nipples was smashed up against a largeish rock, and something sharp jabbed into my hip, but I didn't have the energy to get up.

"You okay?" Jesse the man asked, his voice soft. He gently moved tangled strands of hair away from the sliver of my face that he could see with my nose smashed into the dirt.

I groaned weakly.

"That bad, huh?" His hands were careful on my arms. "Can I carry you?"

I made an angrier noise that came out sounding like a sound a dying animal would make.

He chuckled. "Alright. We'll give it a minute to see if you start feeling better."

His fingers combed more of my hair out of my face, draping it over my back as best as he could.

"Your wolf was testing mine," Jesse explained quietly, filling the silence as we waited.

I was feeling shittier by the moment, so I doubted I'd get better, but wasn't ready to admit that.

"She wanted to know if he could track her through the forest by her scent. It's a pretty common test for wolves—the females want to know that the males can find them should they get separated. When she let my wolf sniff her, she was acknowledging that he passed the test even without knowing her scent intimately."

I would've glared at the dirt if I could open my eyes.

Freakin' wolves, and their freakin' tests.

Couldn't they just get it on in the woods and be done with it?

"You ready to walk to the door?" Jesse checked.

I groaned out a "no".

"You're not going to like this, Tea, but I'm going to have to carry you." His voice remained light, though there was a warning undertone.

I groaned another "no".

"I know it's not ideal, but you need food and sleep to recover. Your body's still adjusting."

Wrestling with my exhaustion, I forced my head up off the ground. My body shook as I struggled to lift my head, but I refused to let it fall.

I'd nearly propped myself up on my forearms when my muscles gave out, and I flopped back to the ground like a bag of rice.

"I'd grab you a blanket or towel, but if I leave, your wolf will probably take over." His voice was thick with apology.

I resigned myself to my fate and shut my eyes tightly, muttering into the dirt, "Alright."

"I'm going to pick you up now."

I braced myself for a feeling of violation.

Jesse's hands found my biceps, and lifted my arms to wrap around his neck. His hands moved to my waist from there, and he lifted me up off the ground without touching me anywhere I wasn't comfortable with.

I guess supernatural strength could come in handy.

Our bare bodies pressed together as he strode in through the back door of the townhouse. There was no hiding my body's effect on his, but neither of us pointed that out.

And by some miracle, the feeling of being violated was completely absent. Instead I felt sort of...taken care of.

It was an eerie feeling, but not an unpleasant one.

Rather than heading up the stairs to drop me in my bed like I was hoping he would, Jesse went to the fridge.

He grabbed a grocery bag and tossed food into it before moving to the stairs, like I'd thought he would to begin with.

We made it to the bathroom, and he carefully set me down inside the tub. I was so weak that my damn head flopped back and smacked the wall.

"Shit. Sorry." Jesse's expression grew strained as he tucked my calves up away from the water before turning it on. It was thoughtful that he protected me from the cold rush, but I wasn't sure how I felt about it considering he had to touch me to do so.

Not that I didn't like being touched by him. I did.

But it was just the principle of the thing.

He plugged the tub when the water ran warm, and then he plopped down on the floor, sitting with his back against the tub so he wasn't looking at me. I could see him, though—all of him.

A relieved breath left him as he opened the bag of food he'd thrown together, and he pulled out a bottle of chocolate milk.

I scowled at it. I hadn't had chocolate milk in ages—especially not the expensive bottled stuff. If I was spending three bucks on a drink, it was a massive Red Bull that was going to buy me at least an extra six hours of serious studying.

Jesse stuck a straw in it and held it out in front of me without looking through the curtain at my body. "Drink."

My scowl deepened.

"You need the calories, Teapot. Drink the milk or I'm climbing into that tub to force-feed it to you."

My eyes flicked to his erection and then to the amused determination in his gaze.

"Yep. No secret that I find you attractive. Make me climb in there, and I'll enjoy it immensely."

With a noise of complaint, I opened my mouth and obeyed his order. The chocolate milk was surprisingly delicious.

My stomach rumbled ferociously as I sipped at the liquid, and my eyebrows lifted.

Jesse chuckled. "I'm going to have to refill this bag before we get you full again."

Unable to give a snarky response, I just kept drinking.

TWENTY-FIVE

JESSE MADE me drink a bottle of chocolate milk, a bottle of strawberry milk, and a bottle of some cinnamon-flavored milk too. I expected to feel full and sloshy when I finished off that much liquid cash, but my stomach was a damn bottomless pit. It was like my body burned through the calories as soon as I consumed them.

"Why do you have so many bottles of milk?" I asked Jesse. Those hadn't been in the fridge when I moved in or before Jesse bit me; there hadn't been bottles of anything.

"The other guys filled our fridge with easy high-calorie foods while I was unconscious," he explained. "It was drilled into us that we'd need to feed our mates a hell of a lot while they adjust to becoming werewolves."

Ah. "So they went with milk? Why not donuts or something?"

"The kind of calories matters. Sugar won't make you stronger; at least milk's got calcium and some protein."

I guess that made sense.

"Can you just throw that towel over your lap?" I asked, trying to gesture toward the towel with my nose since my arms still felt like noodles.

"Why? Am I distracting you?" He gave me a sly grin, reaching for the towel.

"No. I just want you to be comfortable," I drawled. "What about your body would distract me?"

I had eyes; of course he was distracting. The man was built like a damn football player. And not the high school or college kind; the professional ones.

Plus, as he'd said, his dick was huge.

"Don't you worry your pretty little head about my comfort, Tea." He dropped the towel down beside him, not throwing it over his lap. "And here I was, thinking my body would affect you the way yours affects me."

My face heated. "How does my body affect yours?"

He gestured to his erection. "It's pretty obvious."

My blush grew hotter.

"Here." He grabbed a tub of yogurt, and a spoon. "Can you hold the spoon?"

I tried to lift my hand and failed, swearing under my breath as it dropped back to the edge of the tub.

Peeling the lid off the yogurt, Jesse dipped the spoon and lifted it to my lips.

"Don't we have any more chocolate milk?" I huffed, not wanting to be fed like a baby.

"Sure. It's in the fridge, though. I'd be happy to haul your pretty little ass down there if you want to grab it," he offered with another grin.

Dammit.

With a sigh, I opened my lips.

Jesse fed me two yogurts before pulling out the next snack.

A huge jar of peanut butter, and a loaf of bread.

He slathered the bread in peanut butter, slapping together a sandwich and lifting it to my mouth. I reluctantly took a bite, chewing and swallowing quickly.

My stupid stomach rumbled again, just as loud as before.

Jesse cracked another grin. The man's happiness was contagious, even though I wasn't feeling *happy* myself.

By the third peanut butter sandwich, I could finally lift the food to my own freakin' mouth. But, when I finished off the loaf of bread, my stomach was *still* growling.

"I can't afford to be a werewolf," I sighed.

"You can't afford not to eat, either," Jesse countered.

I glared at him.

Why did he have to be right?

"You've got to be hungry too," I said. "Why don't you eat some of that?" I gestured to the bag as he pulled out leftover pizza.

That food, I could get behind.

"I'm built this way for a reason." He gestured to his body again, and I tried not to check him out.

Yeah, I failed.

"The extra food you eat will help you get used to the toll of shifting back and forth while you build up the fat and muscle required to maintain a werewolf body," he explained. "I've heard it takes about a year for a human to finish adjusting, and then the hunger is much more manageable."

I sighed, and then wolfed down what had to be an entire leftover pizza, courtesy of Jesse's packmates. I guessed if you were feeding that many hungry werewolves, one extra pizza wasn't actually that much leftover food.

"How are you feeling?" Jesse asked. "Strong enough to wash up and go down to the kitchen?"

"Yup."

I washed up quickly, and by the time I was clean, was already starving again. I wasn't feeling weak, though, so it was alright.

Jesse followed me out of the bathroom, but I stopped in the doorway to his bedroom first. I gestured toward his closet, and saw the humor in his eyes.

"I was planning on showering after I finish feeding you," he said.

"I'm not eating anything else unless you wear shorts," I warned.

His expression was amused as he strode to his closet, and TBH, I didn't avert my eyes as his chiseled backside stepped into a pair of basketball shorts that hid absolutely nothing.

But, since he'd done as I asked, I followed him to my room next.

He turned around and faced the hallway at my insistence as I slipped into underwear, cotton shorts, and a loose long-sleeve t-shirt. One of my boobs was still feeling sensitive after being crushed against the rock earlier, so a bra was out of the question.

But going braless would keep Jesse on his toes, and I liked keeping him on his toes.

We were in the kitchen a few minutes later, and Jesse pulled a massive chicken pot pie out of the freezer, sticking it in the oven without waiting for it to preheat.

"How long does that need to cook?" I checked, leaning against the counter.

"Not as long as you're going to be up studying." He started some coffee, next, and then grabbed another loaf of bread and the jar of peanut butter. "More sandwiches until then."

I made a face, but really didn't mind. Peanut butter sandwiches weren't as bad as starving, and they were cheap.

Could a person survive on peanut butter sandwiches alone?

I considered it as I walked over to the spot at the kitchen table that I'd turned into a desk.

They had grains, fat, protein...

No fruits and veggies, though.

Eh, peanut butter sandwiches probably wouldn't give me all the nutrients I needed.

I pulled up the assignment list and got to work again. Jesse brought me a tower of peanut butter sandwiches a few minutes later, and I sniffed at them.

"Is that honey?"

"Yep. Now that we're down here, we can eat fancy." He winked.

"Damn, we're cool." I grabbed the top sandwich, and one of the paper towel sheets he'd brought as makeshift napkins.

Jesse was a man after my cheapskate heart.

"Better believe it. Coffee will be up in a few." His fingers skimmed my shoulder before he headed back to the French press and the huge coffee mugs he'd already gotten ready. He had a bit of an addiction to the stuff, but there were worse addictions to have.

BY THE TIME the sun rose, we finally fell asleep on the table together. We'd gone through a grand total of three loaves of bread between the two of us, and devoured the entire chicken pot pie as well as two massive cups of coffee each.

My alarm went off at 6:30, only an hour after we fell asleep.

Jesse shut it off with a groan.

I didn't even lift my head, too tired to turn the damn thing off myself.

As I started falling back asleep, I felt a warm hand on the back of my neck...and another on my arm.

I lifted my head, confused at the contact. My eyes found Jesse passed out on the table, his hands tangled in my hair to rest on my neck and arm. I'd scooted closer to him at some point in the hour I'd been asleep, and my books and papers were scattered haphazardly.

"We should go to bed," I told Jesse.

He mumbled something I couldn't hear.

My fingers found his shoulder, and I shook gently. "Jesse. We need to go upstairs, to our beds."

He mumbled again, and I grabbed his arm. When I pulled it over my shoulder, sliding out of my chair and easing to my feet, he opened his eyes. His head jerked around the room, before tilting to rest against the top of mine as we headed up the stairs.

I hadn't been thinking properly. Jesse was still exhausted from his time in wolf form; I couldn't keep him awake all hours of the night with me. He needed rest. And I needed to look out for him, since he was looking out for me.

I helped him onto his bed, lifting the blankets so he could get his legs beneath him. I'd figured out that werewolves ran a bit warmer than humans, but it was pretty damn cold in the house.

After getting him settled, I tried to step away.

He was already snoring, but sleep-Jesse picked that moment to roll over. He landed up against me, and his arms wrapped around me.

I sighed.

I could've tried to leave... but my wolf probably wouldn't take that well. And since I was still fully-dressed, a few hours of sleep next to him wasn't going to kill me.

I tucked my own legs up underneath the blankets, keeping them a bit away from Jesse's. After setting an alarm, I closed my eyes and was asleep again almost instantly.

LOLA GLASS

. . .

MY ALARM WENT off at 11. I'd only wanted to sleep until 9, but my damned conscience made me give Jesse the extra two hours. Since I couldn't leave his side without my wolf taking over, I'd need to wake him up if I was going to get back to my homework.

I woke up curled against Jesse, my front to his. His breathing was steady, his body so damn warm I wanted to melt into him.

I'd never spent a night with a man before, but something about waking up pressed against those muscles made me feel a bit fluttery.

"Jesse?" I wiggled, but was pretty much completely trapped. "Jesse." I rocked against him.

His erection throbbed against my pelvis, and I stopped abruptly.

Shit.

WTF was I thinking?

"Jesse." I nudged his chin with the top of my head.

His lips curved upward in a hint of a sleepy smile.

"Damn you!" I hissed. "You're not even asleep!"

"Your alarm was loud," he said drowsily. "And you seemed like you were having fun trying to escape."

My face burned. "I wasn't trying to—" I made a frustrated noise. "Just let go of me." I shoved his arms off of me, getting off the bed and striding toward the bathroom. "Stay where you are."

I could see his feet sticking out the bottom of the comforter on his bed with the bathroom door open, so I used the facilities without him standing in the doorway for once.

When I was done, I headed back to the bedroom and crossed my arms. He had stayed where he was, looking entirely relaxed with his arms behind his head as he watched me.

"I've got to get back to studying, so I need you to get out of bed," I warned.

"Alright." He stayed where he was.

"Come on." I waved him toward the stairs.

"Easy, Teapot. We can take a couple minutes to relax."

I rolled my eyes. "Relaxing is for people who don't get shit done."

He chuckled. "Just come here."

I reluctantly trudged over to the bed, only because I was pretty confident that he wouldn't get up unless I did. "What?"

"Come on." He patted the mattress beside him.

"You do know I didn't get in this bed earlier intending to cuddle with you, right?" I checked. "We're not a thing."

"I'm aware." There was humor in his eyes. "Just get in."

TWENTY-SIX

WITH A DRAMATIC SIGH, I slid under the blankets and lowered myself to my back on the mattress. There was a good foot of space between Jesse and I—something I didn't particularly like, but did feel was necessary.

I wasn't going to be the kidnapped, mail-ordered, Stockholm-Syndromed bride, after all.

"Close your eyes," Jesse instructed.

I opened my mouth to argue.

"Tea, close your mouth and shut your eyes. You know I'm not going to grab your tits or anything."

Did I know that?

Yeah, I knew that. He'd been a perfect gentleman, despite his body's obvious reaction to me.

My eyes closed.

"Where do you see yourself in ten years?" he asked.

"Working in a hospital. Living next door to my mom. Buying her the shoes she stares at in the store window and taking her out to eat; shit she never could afford when I was a kid because kids are so expensive," I answered automatically.

"What else?" he asked.

I opened my eyes, shooting him a frown. "What do you mean, what else?"

"What else do you see yourself doing in ten years? Having a kid of your own? Learning to paint? Going back to school for your master's degree? You're a planner; you must have some idea of your future other than financial stability."

I shot him an irritated glare. "This is what you call relaxing?"

"Yep."

"You're obnoxious." I turned my head back to the ceiling, shutting my eyes again. And though I knew I didn't have to, I decided to play Jesse's little game.

What did I want out of life, other than not having to worry about money?

My mind went back to the past month. To the way it had felt when I sat on the couch, studying, with Wolf Jesse snuggled up against my feet. For no reason that made logical sense, it was so much more enjoyable than studying alone.

Everything had been more enjoyable with Jesse the Wolf than when I was alone.

"I think I'd like to get married, at some point," I finally said. "Or maybe just find a partner to share my life with. Someone to talk to when I get home from work, and text when something funny happens."

"And snuggle at night?"

I shot Jesse another glare. "I know what you're doing. You want me to see that having a mate is a blessing, just like your mom was trying to tell me. I understand that it's special, and that at some point I'll probably be glad that your wolf picked me, but—" I cut myself off when his hand landed on my arm.

"That's not what I'm doing, Tea."

I glared, waiting for him to clarify.

"I'm not trying to manipulate you. I asked because I wanted to know your answer, not because I want you to think I *am* the answer." He paused. "Though on second thought, I could be."

I smacked him on the chest with the back of my hand, and he chuckled. "I was kidding."

"Sure you were." Drawing my hand back, I placed it on my abdomen with the other one.

"We could be good together, you know. I've seen the way you look at me, and you know how I look at you. We could—"

"We've known each other for like three days, Jesse. I get that you watched me through your wolf for a couple of months, but I'm not jumping into a relationship with someone I just met regardless of any werewolf magic." I slid out of the bed. "I need to catch up on my homework."

Jesse leaned across the bed and caught my wrist in a light grip. "That's fair. You need time. I get that. But I'd like to revisit this conversation, at some point."

"When the semester ends, you can bring it back up. There's a decent chance I'll shoot it down again, but you can try. Until then, please just leave it alone." I headed to the doorway without his confirmation, waiting for him to get ready to go downstairs.

He stepped into the bathroom, remaining where I could see bits of him as he moved, and came back out a few minutes later wearing a t-shirt along with his shorts.

We walked down the stairs together, everything made a bit less comfortable by the conversation we'd just had.

"You want coffee?" Jesse asked, as I sat down at the kitchen table.

"Sure." I opened my laptop, massaging my temples as the screen lit up.

Damn, I wished I had a Red Bull to drink.

Jesse turned on music while he started the coffee, then grabbed two dozen eggs and set them on the counter. The eggs were followed by a pack of bacon and some bread—for toast, I assumed.

"I don't usually eat breakfast," I reminded Jesse.

My stomach growled as he shot me a warning look.

"Fine," I muttered, looking back at my computer screen and pulling up the list of shit I still needed to do.

"Consider me your werewolf dietician and personal chef," Jesse said, turning back to the stove. "Most girls could only dream of having their own were-chef, but you're lucky enough to have me."

I snorted. "Most girls would run screaming from a *were-chef*."

"Haven't you heard of paranormal romance books? If girls like sparkly vampires, you'd better believe they like muscular werewolves cooking them eggs."

He didn't turn around to see the grin tugging my lips upward.

"Who said you were muscular?" I countered.

"I do own a mirror, Teapot. Doesn't take much more than a mirror and a pair of eyes to deduce that when you've got this to work with." He gestured to his body from the side.

"I don't know why men think it's attractive to talk about their muscles. Obviously, they're there." I gestured to his body, like he had. "You know it, I know it."

"You asked."

"I was teasing you, *Kettle*." I rolled my eyes, opening the document I had set up for a particular assignment on my computer. Two could play the nickname game. If he wanted to call me Teapot, you'd better believe I'd be calling him Kettle.

"It seems like every time I ask an attractive guy what he likes to do, do you know what he says?" I asked, mostly ranting to myself at that point. "Go to the gym. They think that's an interesting hobby, but what girl wants to date someone whose idea of a good time is working out?"

"A girl whose idea of a good time is working out?" Jesse suggested.

It took a minute to realize he was answering my rhetorical question...

And in an interesting way.

"No one's idea of a good time is working out."

"Sure it is. There are plenty of people who enjoy the way they feel when they get their heartrate up." He continued cooking eggs, arguing with me casually, in a way that I hated to admit I loved.

"If this is where you tell me your favorite thing to do is work out, I'm moving."

He shot me a grin over his shoulder. "I don't personally work out. I'd rather read a book."

"Ditto." I tried to focus on my assignment, but now that Jesse had gotten me ranting, I had a million things to say. "Why do guys think it's sexy to say they love working out, though? Is it supposed to make us think of sex or something? Because when a guy tells me his favorite hobby is the gym, I immediately think he's a few brain cells short of intelligent."

Jesse laughed. The sound was enough to nearly make me smile.

"I'm sure they say that to you because it sounds more manly than admitting they play video games in all their spare time or telling you they're really into watching medical dramas. Exercise seems like a safe answer. And it probably works with a decent number of girls, if they keep using it."

I scoffed. "Video games and TV bingeing are way more interesting."

"To you," he pointed out. "Not everyone is you."

"Thanks, Captain Obvious."

"You're welcome, Miss Old Insult."

"Old insult? Captain Obvious is a classic," I protested.

"It's not."

"Then what's the new version of it?"

Jesse shrugged. "No idea. I never claimed to be hip—I just said it's outdated."

"Well that's not exactly helpful, is it?" I gave him an exasperated look.

"I never claimed to be helpful." He walked over with my mug of coffee and a slight grin.

"You say that, as you serve me coffee and make me eggs." I took the mug, curling my fingers around the warm glass.

"Technically I'm doing that for me. If I don't feed you, you're going to keep bullying me." His widening grin told me he was teasing. "And if I don't feed you then eventually you'll starve to death because of your terrible eating habits. Assuming you starve to death, I'd be out a mate, which would mean a life of loneliness."

"Wow. Thanks for pointing that out." I nodded, sipping the coffee in my mug. I'd started to actually like the taste of it—something I hadn't expected could happen. "I'll remind myself of that next time you try to cuddle with me."

He nodded. "Good call."

Twenty minutes of egg-cracking and stirring later, he set a popcorn bowl full of scrambled eggs in front of me. Bacon and toast were tucked up against the sides of the bowl, framing the assload of eggs.

"This is what I've come to?" I asked in despair, as my stomach growled loudly.

"Yup. You can thank me for that, too." He sat beside me with his own bowl of eggs. Though it was large, it was probably a third of the size of mine. "Dig in, Teapot."

TWENTY-SEVEN

THE NEXT FEW days were a whirl of food, studying, school, and sass.

The sass was pretty much just teasing banter between Jesse and I. We could go back and forth for an hour about something neither of us was even really passionate about—we just liked to argue.

But the problem with our constant banter?

It made me like Jesse way more than I should have, considering we'd only known each other for a week.

I ignored the liking and tried to focus on school and eating enough so that my body would stop going into panic mode when my damn wolf took over. Staying close to Jesse, I managed to keep her at bay until Wednesday.

We were on campus, walking to my last class.

"That was the most boring lecture we've ever had from that guy," Jesse yawned.

"You've only been to three of his lectures," I pointed out.

"Luckily."

Jesse went to open the door just as some girl pushed it open. He stepped back in time to avoid being whacked by the thing, but the girl's huge eyes went wide and her lips formed a perfect O shape.

She was gorgeous; perfect makeup, winged eyeliner, definite lip-fillers and who knew what other face-work done. And she was wearing a tight mini-skirt and a bandeau bra that somehow managed to make her curves look curvier.

I wasn't the girl who envied other chicks.

My wolf?

Apparently, she was another story.

"I'm so sorry!" the girl gushed, stepping up to Jesse and putting both hands on his chest.

My wolf surged forward, and I barely bit back a scream of pain. I crashed into Jesse's back, knocking him directly into the girl as I tried to figure out how to shove my wolf away.

Shifting in the middle of campus while there were a bunch of people around? Not a good way to stay alive.

The girl grabbed his biceps, pressing every inch of her front to his. She was taking full advantage of the situation, and I didn't freakin' blame her. Jesse was a piece of eye-candy that even someone who didn't eat sugar wouldn't be able to resist.

I stifled a scream as my spine felt like it cracked.

"Excuse me." Jesse's voice was more brittle than I'd ever heard it as he extricated himself from the girl's arms and turned to me.

My eyes pinched shut as I tried to breathe through another sharp spasm of pain in my back.

Jesse smoothly slid an arm around my waist, the other taking my hand and easing my arm over his shoulder. We "walked" quickly to the edge of the campus, toward the thick forest that would hide us from view of the school's cameras and curious human eyes.

"Walked," because Jesse was legitimately holding *all* of my weight.

"Push back at her the way she pushes at you," Jesse spoke calmly, his voice quiet.

"I'm trying," I said through clenched teeth. "What the hell is wrong with her?"

"She's possessive, same as the rest of us. I don't wear your mark, so she's going to attack anyone who tries to claim me in any way."

"That girl only ran into you."

"To a wolf trying to choose a mate, anyone of the other gender is a threat. You saw how my wolf reacted when you kissed our pack members."

A small shriek tore through me as another wave of pain stabbed my spine.

"Plus, she was grabbing me like a damn piece of meat," Jesse sounded annoyed. "Can you imagine if I ran into some chick and grabbed her tit the way she was grabbing my chest?"

A strangled noise came from my throat as the wolf pushed harder.

"Stop talking about it," I begged, my knees buckling. Jesse kept holding my weight, not fazed by my loss of strength.

"We're almost to the forest. Think about something calming. The sound of a waterfall—the way the trees rustle in the wind."

"River rocks," I struggled to inhale.

Jesse looked confused. "Sure. River rocks. Whatever the hell that smells like."

I snorted, then wheezed.

We reached the trees, and Jesse swept me into his arms as I lost the fight with my wolf. He hauled me further into the forest at a jog as my body changed, bones cracking and reforming.

I buried my face against his chest, biting down on his coat to stifle my screams.

"I've got to get these clothes off you," he murmured, as he slowed to a jog and then stopped altogether. "I'll be quick."

He lowered me to a less-snowy part of the ground, then his fingers quickly worked the fabric off my skin. My body contorted painfully, and I forced my hand to my mouth to hide my scream.

The forest hid us from everyone else's sight, but we were still close to the campus. If I started screaming, someone would come looking to figure out what was going on.

Jesse dropped his coat and tugged his shirt up over his head, balling it up. He carefully moved my hand from my mouth and tucked his shirt in its place. It was a weird thing to do, but I bit down automatically when the next crack of pain hit me, and I understood why he'd done it. It was sweet, really.

"I'm sorry." Jesse's fingers stroked my scalp, brushing beads of sweat away from my hairline. "Just try to breathe. Let her take over, and it'll be easier."

I warred with the wolf, trying to withdraw from the fight but failing. My hatred for being controlled was too strong; I couldn't stop trying to prevent her from taking over.

She was intruding on my body. I'd existed long before her; I should've been the one in control.

My body shifted in one last sharp crack, and my scream of pain became a howl.

"Shhh." Jesse's arms wrapped around my wolf, tucking her up against his bare chest. His ass was in the snow, but he didn't seem to care.

He stroked her head and neck, and every one of his touches calmed her.

"It's alright, Teagan," he murmured. "You're my mate, and I've claimed you. I'm not interested in any other human or wolf. You're it for me, remember?"

The words pacified her a little.

Until she snuggled up against his neck.

Something caught her attention and pissed her off in a heartbeat.

"Shit." Jesse muttered as my wolf snarled. "She touched my skin, huh?"

The wolf snapped her teeth at the air before sprinting through the forest.

I heard Jesse swearing as he sprinted after her, but he was much slower than my wolf.

She shot through the trees, her paws landing on concrete in only moments. I had no freakin' clue what she was doing, but I had a feeling I wasn't going to like it.

Though, that one was common sense more than anything. When had I ever liked losing control of my own damn body?

My wolf's eyes landed on the girl who had run into Jesse, and horror bloomed within me.

She wanted to eliminate her competition.

I banged against my mental cage, trying to figure out how the wolf took control from me so I could replicate it, but the walls holding me were solid.

Screams rang out from the girls grouped around the chatty, touchy-feely one who'd grabbed Jesse, when the saw my pissed-off wolf, who was out for blood.

She headed right for them.

"Run!" someone screamed.

My wolf dove toward the girl.

The girl's scream pierced the air, a noise that would linger with me for a long time, as her arms lifted to protect her face and throat.

My wolf's teeth sliced through the skin on her arm and broke through bone. The crunch would've been enough to make me nauseous, but her blood-curdling scream made me feel like a monster.

Her good hand clutched her broken and torn arm, lowering as she kicked and kneed my wolf.

Wolf Jesse knocked into my side, and my beast snarled at the male who'd kept her from her prey.

Said prey was already running toward the nearest building, thick mascara tears running down her face as she sobbed.

I wanted to cry too, but couldn't.

Wolf Jesse nudged me toward the woods as someone came running toward us with what looked like a dog collar attached to a pole.

The sight of the tool scared my wolf a bit, and Jesse's nudging and growling was growing more desperate by the second. She finally got the memo that those people were a threat to her, and booked it back to the forest.

Shouts followed her and Wolf Jesse into the trees. He took the lead, taking us back to our clothes.

Shifting took him no more than two minutes—he was faster than me, and seemed to be in much less pain swapping forms than I had been in.

When he was in skin, he grabbed my wolf's face. "I need you to shift back," he urged. "Those guys are looking for wolves, or at least massive dogs. You need to be in human form to stay alive."

My wolf growled. I wasn't sure if it was a "no" or a "that's bullshit," or an, "I'm growling at you to say thanks."

"Come on, Teagan. I've protected you and marked you; you're mine to protect. Trust me on this, and stop fighting."

My wolf finally gave in.

She withdrew quickly, and I began to shift back.

The pain was excruciating. By the time I made it back to human form, there were tear streaks down my eyes, and my lashes were probably clumpy from the combination of crying and what little mascara I'd put on that morning.

"Here." Jesse quickly helped me into my clothes, then put his on minus the bitten t-shirt, and then slipped my arm over his shoulder and eased me to my feet.

"I can walk," I told him quietly.

"I know." He released me, bending down to dunk the t-shirt in a handful of snow. "Wait." He caught my arm, stopping me before I could walk away.

When I stopped, he lifted the snowy shirt to my face.

I cringed away. "What are you doing?"

"You've got some blood." His voice was steady, his eyes kind.

I lifted my hand to my face and pulled it away. When I saw the red staining my fingers, a strangled cry forced its way out.

"Shh." His arm wrapped around my waist, his other hand quickly cleaning my face with the snowy shirt.

"I'm a monster." My eyes burned, my heart beating wildly. "You turned me into a fucking monster."

"I'm sorry, Tea. Really. If there was any way to—"

"Stop. Just stop. No more excuses, or reasoning. You lulled me into thinking this is safe and normal, but it's not. I'm a monster, Jesse." I pulled out of his grip, and he let me go.

TWENTY-EIGHT

I STRODE AWAY, and heard footsteps as Jesse followed me. He was silent for the most part, but there was no denying his presence.

My mind churned as I struggled to come up with a plan as to what I was going to do next.

What *was* there to do next?

I was stuck living at Jesse's house, and was the host to a practically-parasitic wolf who could snatch my body any time she wanted. I was constantly starving as I tried to adapt physically to the wolf within me, but didn't have the money to pay for the food I'd need to keep adapting without Jesse.

Maybe if I could figure out how to control my wolf, I could get away from Jesse after the mating shit was over. Maybe I could learn how to be a lone wolf or something. Jesse's mom had said it wasn't possible, that our wolves would constantly seek each other out, but why would I trust her? She was as much a monster as the rest of them.

The rest of *us*.

We ran into the animal control guys as we exited the forest. Jesse stepped up to my side, his fingers slipping between mine. I wanted to pull away, but was pretty sure I knew what he was doing.

"What were you doin' out there?" one of the animal control guys asked, his gaze on us suspicious.

Jesse smirked at the men. "Just enjoying the fresh air alone together."

One of them glanced at me, undoubtedly taking in my messy hair and clothes. Awareness flooded their gazes.

"In the snow?" another of the guys asked.

"Everyone's got their kinks." The first guy shrugged. "Did you see any wolves out there?"

Shit. They knew we were wolves, not dogs.

"No, sorry. We were a little busy." Jesse's hand slid out of mine, so his arm could drape over my shoulder. "Are we good to go?"

"Sure. Just be careful; there are some rabid wolves out here," one of the guys warned.

Jesse and I nodded like we were scared, and headed toward the cars.

I removed his arm from my shoulder as I strode toward his vehicle. My fists clenched at my sides as I tried to come up with an alternative to the shitshow that was my life.

I couldn't come up with a single damn one.

We drove home in silence, other than the music playing quietly from the speakers. Jesse was trying to give me time to work through my thoughts, I assumed, but there was no *working through* happening.

Only fierce frustration building.

"Let's have dinner with the pack tonight," Jesse said as we parked in the garage.

He hadn't brought it up since the last time I shot him down, but I'd known it was only a matter of time.

"Fine." I didn't know why I was agreeing to it; my life had gone to hell because of their damn pack.

"Don't sound so enthusiastic, Teapot." Jesse patted my knee.

"Don't touch me." My voice came out harsher than I intended.

He withdrew his hand, his eyebrows colliding as he frowned.

"You made me a monster, Jesse. I get that you didn't have a choice, but you're still the reason I am what I am now. That's not something I can just forget and let go."

He nodded, raking a hand through his hair before buckling his seatbelt. "Let's get you some food."

His voice was strained, the way it usually got when he was horny. But this time, there was no lust involved.

I didn't care to know what emotion had replaced it.

We went inside, and I sat down at the kitchen table. My hands pulled my laptop out of my bag on autopilot, as Jesse stepped up to the fridge.

Instead of opening it, he reached up to the top and grabbed the envelope still resting up there.

He brought it over to me, setting it down on the table in front of me. "I know money can't buy back the life you had, but this is all I've got to offer. Take it; it's yours."

He walked back to the fridge, and I stared at the envelope for a minute.

Taking the money was a betrayal, wasn't it?

It meant accepting my fate as a werewolf, and accepting that I was going to be spending my life with Jesse whether I liked it or not.

I didn't want to accept anything.

I didn't want to decide anything.

If I was resigned to being controlled by an animal, and living with someone I didn't choose, my life wasn't really mine anyway. So what was the point of any of it?

I left the envelope of money on the table, and got up to walk to the bathroom. If I was away from Jesse, my wolf would take control and I wouldn't have to think or feel as much.

She wanted my life; she could have it.

I stepped into the bathroom and waited for her to take over.

She didn't make a peep.

Closing the bathroom door behind me, I waited for her to get angry that I was separated from Jesse. I waited for her to rip control out of my hands so she could make sure I did what she wanted.

But she didn't.

Minutes passed. My emotions grew more numb, and I slipped back out of the bathroom. There was a plate of food on the counter in front of my chair. I left it there, and instead picked up the envelope of cash. Jesse was no longer in the kitchen.

My fingers found the car keys he'd left on the hook, and I stepped into the garage. My bag of cash was clutched to my chest, and I held the keys in a death-grip.

I needed an escape. Freedom. A way out.

But I was still a monster. There was nowhere I could escape to and still prevent my wolf from hurting innocent people.

Except maybe a bar.

Pulling up maps on my phone, I searched the town. I wasn't twenty-one yet, but considering our digestive systems worked differently, maybe werewolves didn't care how old you were.

Pulling out of the garage, my heart pounded as I waited for my wolf to take over. If she took over while I was driving, I assumed I could pull over before the pain became unbearable.

She didn't take over, though.

I didn't feel her at all.

The robotic voice on my map app gave me directions, and I followed them in silence. The numbness within me seemed to grow.

I parked in front of the bar a few minutes later. There were cars outside, but the lot wasn't full.

I pulled a chunk of cash out of the envelope before shoving the envelope under the seat. Even feeling numb, I wasn't about to risk thousands of dollars.

Tucking the wad of cash in my bra, I slid out of the car and headed inside the bar.

No one turned to look at me when I entered. It felt good not to be noticed; it made me feel normal.

My wolf was still absent, leaving me to my misery.

I sat down at an empty stool on the edge of the bar, and the bartender made his way over to me. "What can I get you?"

"Something strong." I had no idea what I would drink; I wasn't one of those girls who went to parties or tried to find ways around the rules. I'd had alcohol every now and then, but only drank a little, and only cheap wine with my mom.

"You got an ID?" he checked.

"Nope." My ID was in my backpack. Even if I'd had it, he didn't want to see it.

"A mate bite?"

My head jerked in a nod. I stood, tugging my shirt up just enough to show him part of the bite on my hip.

"Alright, something strong coming right up."

Relief flooded me as I sat back down on the stool.

Apparently a bite mark was as good as an ID in Moon Ridge.

The door opened, and a little bell jingled. I didn't turn around; no one had turned around when I went inside, so that was probably the way people did things in the bar. And I wanted to do things right so they didn't kick me out, because Jesse's house was the only alternative.

A minute later, someone sat beside me.

I didn't glance at them. "Go home, Jesse."

"I'd think you could recognize your own mate." Ford's rumble met my ears instead of Jesse's smooth timbre. "We don't exactly look alike."

The bartender set a drink down in front of me, and I thanked him.

"I hadn't heard you found a mate," the bartender told Ford, looking at me a bit differently.

"She's Jesse's," Ford responded, eyeing the glass now in my hands. "Are you twenty-one yet?"

"Yep." I lifted it to my lips and took a small drink. The liquid nearly came right back up.

Shit, that burned.

The bartender walked away, coming back a minute later with a drink for Ford. Ford thanked him, but didn't pick it up.

"You know alcohol doesn't work well on us, right?" he asked, not unkindly.

I hadn't known that.

Should've realized it, but hadn't.

"Don't care," I said, taking another sip of my drink.

Ford nodded. "You get in a fight with Jesse?"

"I figured he'd told you what happened." I didn't look at him.

We hadn't really gotten in a fight. Jesse and I fought all the time, and it was always playful. This was something else.

Something worse.

So if he was asking about a fight, he didn't know what had happened on campus.

"He showed up and tried to steal my car. I'd have given it to him, but he's a shit driver." Ford shrugged. "Didn't say a damn word why, but when we got here he asked me to come in and check on you."

I scoffed. "I don't need a babysitter."

"How about a friend?"

My scoff vanished.

I drank the rest of the alcohol. It burned, but I hoped it would take the edge off. So far, I wasn't feeling any different at all.

The bartender refilled my drink, and Ford and I were silent until he walked away again.

"Some girl hit on Jesse. The wolf snatched my body and nearly killed her. Her arm looked like..." I shook my head hard, shuddering at the images in my memory.

Ford nodded slowly, not saying anything still.

"I didn't want this," I told him. "I didn't want to be a monster. Jesse made me into this." I gestured toward my chest. "There was blood on my face. *Human* blood." I shuddered again. "I just...can't."

"Sounds like a shitty day." Ford finally picked up his drink, sipping at it.

"That's an understatement." I lifted my glass back to my lips and choked down some more of the burning liquid.

"And now your wolf's fine being away from Jesse?"

"Apparently. I keep trying to get her to take over, but she won't."

Ford didn't say anything for a long moment. I was content with the quiet, until I glanced outside the window at the front of the bar.

My gaze caught on an agitated Jesse, pacing the parking lot like the damn road was out to get him.

"What's he freaking out about?" I asked Ford.

I was the one who'd been turned into a monster; I was the one who'd lost my life as I knew it.

"Your wolf shouldn't be alright with being away from him right now. If she's not insisting on being with him, it means she's done chasing him. If she's done chasing, she's either decided he's the one or she's decided he's not. Given what happened earlier, I'd assume he's thinking it's the second one."

My mind spun. "What happens if she doesn't want him?"

"He'll spend his life alone. Your wolf will eventually chase another male, and the other guy's hunt will follow her chase."

So if not Jesse, there would be someone else for me.

Another damn werewolf match.

But…

I couldn't do that; not to Jesse. He'd turned me into a monster, but he hadn't really had a choice in the matter. He wasn't a complete bastard. When my emotions ran high, it was easy to blame him for everything, but deep down I knew that there wasn't anyone to blame.

It was just… fate.

And honestly, I liked Jesse. He was a good man, and a good friend.

I'd never had a friend like him before. One I could fight playfully with, one who wasn't offended by my sometimes-harsh jokes. One who'd call me on my shit and liked it when I called him on his.

"How will we know which it is?" I asked, my voice lower than it had been.

"She'll bite him soon, if she chooses him. If she doesn't, she'll attack him the next time he touches either of you."

I swallowed the rest of my drink. "How evil would it be to leave Jesse to his own thoughts for another ten minutes?"

Ford shot me a serious look. "If your wolf's decided he's not worthy, his entire life will be fucked, Tea. This isn't a joke for him. A werewolf without a mate usually goes insane before he turns thirty."

Shit.

Regardless of any lingering resentment, I couldn't let that happen to him.

Jesse was too brilliant, and kind, and fun, to lose his mind because of me.

With a groan, I stuffed my hand into my bra and pulled out the wad of cash. Trying to decide how much the total would be for the two drinks, I frowned.

I knew nothing about the price of alcohol.

Ford reached over and plucked a twenty-dollar bill out of my pile. He set it on the bar, but made no move to get up.

"I'll wait in here in case Jesse needs a ride back," he told me.

I felt a bit insulted by the neutrality in his tone, but then again, we weren't really friends.

"Great." I strode toward the door.

TWENTY-NINE

JESSE'S EYES tracked my every movement as I crossed the parking lot.

My heart sped up at the intense look he wore. He was always easygoing and calm; I'd never seen him look like he was feeling so much.

As I approached him, I tried to come up with something to say. A good way to bring up the topic, or the right words to apologize for the harsh things I'd said and the stress I'd obviously caused him.

But all thoughts of apologies fled my mind when Jesse covered the remaining distance between us in three steps.

With one rough movement, he crushed my body to his and pressed his lips to mine.

It took my mind a minute to catch up, but when I did, I reacted. Jesse didn't know much about kissing, but a tiny press of the lips meant nothing to me.

And I wanted this kiss to mean something.

My tongue teased the entrance to his mouth, and he opened for me without hesitation. When I tasted him without reservation, he mimicked the action until he was just as confident as I was.

My hands found his head, holding his face to mine as I met him stroke for stroke. I'd been kissed before, and I had kissed people before, but this was nothing like that.

His lips were on mine, and our tongues warred the way our words always did. Our bodies moved together, as one. His hands were on my hips, mine in his hair, our mouths and bodies practically locked together as we ravaged each other.

A car's horn honked, and our lips tore apart, our eyes colliding with those of the vehicle's driver.

I didn't recognize him, but he looked amused.

Jesse drew me back a few steps, toward our car. I wasn't sure when I'd started considering it mine too, but I did.

Jesse waved at the guy in the vehicle, and the guy drove through the space in the road that we'd been blocking.

Letting out a long, harsh breath, he crushed me to his chest and held me tightly.

"Wow," I breathed.

I'd never been kissed like that.

Hell, I'd never *felt* like that.

And now that I had... I wasn't sure I could go back to *not* feeling it.

"I'm so damn glad your wolf still wants me," Jesse said, clutching me against him.

He was so glad...what?

That my wolf still wanted him?

Had we not just experienced the same life-altering, earth-shattering kiss?

Holy hell, what if he hadn't felt the same way I did?

My defenses rose, and I stepped away from Jesse.

He let me go.

His expression was one of relief. "Sorry, I probably shouldn't have kissed you. It was desperate, and stupid."

I glared at him. "Yeah, it was."

And apparently, it hadn't been the same life-changing kiss for him.

"But at least you know you won't live your whole life alone anymore." I spun around, striding to Jesse's car. "Since apparently my wolf has decided to bite you."

Dread flooded me.

After my wolf bit him, we'd be consumed with lust.

The Climax, Rocco had said.

The last thing I wanted was to have heaps of sex with someone while knowing that it wasn't as big of a deal for him as it was for me. He cared about me because I was his mate—nothing more.

What a freakin' shit show.

"Based on the display back there, I assume you're not going to be needing a ride back," Ford drawled, striding to his car.

Jesse looked at me, and then Ford looked at me too when neither of us said anything right away.

"Give him a ride back. I have plans," I lied, sliding into the driver's seat.

When I glanced back at Jesse, he looked... confused.

While I pulled out of the parking lot, I called my only real friend other than Jesse. And things between us were so complicated that it wasn't just plain ole' friendship, even if he was probably my best friend. The phone rang, and Ebony picked up on the second ring.

"Hello?"

"Hey, Ebony. It's Tea." I let out a slow breath. "I miss hanging out. Can you meet for dinner, or ice cream? I'll buy."

The wad of cash in my bra weighed a hell of a lot more than it should've.

Probably because it was Jesse's money, not mine.

She hesitated. I'd lived with her long enough to know that school always, always came first for her. But she didn't get out much, and she and I had chatted for at least a few minutes most days over the year we'd lived together. We weren't insanely close, but we were friends, and we had each other's backs.

"Sure. Yeah. I've only got an hour or so, but we could do Taco Bell or something."

I'd have to order a shitload of food there, and Ebony would know something was different. If we went to a sandwich shop, the food would fill me for a solid half an hour and I could order another one or two after my friend left.

"How about Subway?" I checked. It wasn't the sub shop I'd worked at, but I didn't want to go back there.

"Sure. That sounds great," she agreed. "What time?"

"Half an hour?"

She said she'd be there, and we both hung up.

My mind spun as I drove down the dirt road I'd once walked. It had been so alien to me then, but now I knew it like the back of my hand. I knew which potholes to avoid, and which ones I could hit without slowing down. I knew when the turns were coming up, and where the wildlife tended to cross.

I forced myself to face the facts, to confront my emotions.

I had feelings for Jesse.

I liked him.

Liked him, liked him, in a way I hadn't liked anyone before.

But his feelings for me...they weren't real. They were created and forced by his wolf's decision to choose me. And for him, it wasn't a choice.

He could be with me, or he could be alone.

He hadn't even been fazed after our kiss. It was like it hadn't affected him at all.

But the same kiss had woken me up to my feelings for him. It had forced me to realize that I couldn't be just friends with Jesse. We had too much chemistry, too much in common, too much *fun*.

Yet at the same time, I didn't know if he had any *real* feelings for me. What if everything he'd done since we met was just because he didn't want to live his life alone?

My churning mind kept right on rolling until I got to Subway.

Getting out of the car, I went inside and looked around. Ebony was usually early for things, and yep, she was sitting at a table near the door.

She stood when I came inside, and gave me a big hug. "It's been too long," she said warmly.

"I know, we need to get together more often." I gave her as much of a smile as I could muster.

We ordered our subs, and took them back to our table to eat. The place wasn't too busy, but we weren't the only ones there.

The door opened, and I glanced to the side as two large bodies entered.

I tried not to react when Jesse and Ford walked past us without a second glance, headed up to the counter. I should've known they'd follow; Jesse had probably assumed I had plans with a male friend or something. The guys all thought I was a slut after all, since I'd kissed a couple of them.

"Damn," Ebony's eyes tracked the men.

The wolf in me stirred.

Shit.

How had I already forgotten about her bitchy jealous tendencies?

Ebony wasn't a flirt though, and she wasn't looking for a relationship. I knew she had a guy friend she'd spend the night with once a week or so, but I had never met him. They weren't *dating*.

She peeled her eyes off the guys and met my gaze. "Football players, maybe?"

"Probably," I agreed.

If Jesse came over, I'd have to admit to knowing him. Maybe I'd call him my roommate or something. But since he and Ford hadn't acknowledged me, I wasn't thinking I'd have to do that.

She made a face. "Why do all the hot ones have to be jocks?"

I smiled. "You took the words right out of my mouth."

My smile faded as I watched Ford and Jesse find seats on the opposite side of the place.

Not all of the hot ones were jocks.

"So how are you doing? How's your new place?" Ebony asked me, unwrapping her sandwich.

"It's nice," I admitted. "I have a roommate, so rent isn't bad."

It wasn't bad at all, considering it was free.

And I needed to talk to Jesse about paying my half of the bills, since he'd given me his cash stash.

"Oh, nice. Is she cool?"

I nearly lied and said yes. But, then I remembered why I'd asked her to go out in the first place. I needed someone to talk to, to help me figure out my feelings.

"It's a he, actually." I grimaced. "The guy over there."

Ebony's eyes flicked to the table, where Jesse and Ford were eating without facing us. "Which one?"

"The one with his back to the register."

She scanned both guys again. "Wow." She turned back to me. "How do you like living with a guy?"

"He's usually a good roommate. I'm just... struggling."

"Why? Do you have feelings for him?"

I made a face.

"Damn. You falling for a jock... I never saw that coming."

"He's not a jock. He's majoring in software engineering, and from what I can tell, he's a damned genius."

Ebony's eyebrows lifted upward. "And he looks like that? Shit. Girl, scoop him up." She glanced at the guys again. "Is his friend single?"

My lips lifted in a slight smile. "No. Sorry." From what I knew, the werewolves didn't date.

"Dammit. If he gets single, tell me."

I nodded.

"So what's the problem, then? You're a hot nerd, he's a hot nerd... Seems like a recipe for a successful relationship."

"I'm not sure his feelings for me are real," I admitted, lowering my voice so I could be sure Jesse and Ford didn't hear me.

She frowned. "You think he just wants in your pants?"

I shook my head. "No. I think he only wants me because I'm there and available."

Ebony nodded. "I can understand that. But I don't necessarily think it's a bad thing."

I wasn't sure what she was trying to say.

"Whenever two people fall in love, they only do so because they both show up for each other. If he shows up for you and you show up for him, why does anything else matter?"

I bit my lip. "But what if I feel more for him than he does for me?"

"Someone has to be the one who loves more." She shrugged. "As long as you've got respect and loyalty, why does it matter who loves who more? A relationship isn't a contest."

Well, I guess that made sense.

The topic shifted to our classes, and we talked about professors and exams until Ebony said her time was up. She thanked me for dinner, and we walked to her car together.

"I miss you, you know. If you ever want to come back to the dorm room, you know it's still yours too," she said, hugging me tightly.

"I know." I gave her a faint smile. "But I'm happy where I am."

"Good," she said simply, then slid into her car. "Let's do this again next week."

"Wednesday night?" I checked.

She nodded, and it was set in stone.

I considered going back into the sub shop, but then decided I wanted the extra time in the car, alone with my thoughts.

THIRTY

OUR CONVERSATION REPLAYED in my mind on the way back to Moon Ridge. Ford and Jesse followed close behind in Ford's sports car, but I'd figured they would and it didn't distract me.

The words that caught in my mind were my own.

I'd told Ebony, "I'm happy where I am."

That was the phrase that seemed to play on repeat in my mind.

I'm happy where I am.

I considered it. The words had come out automatically; I hadn't thought of them as a lie.

And if they weren't a lie, were they the truth?

Was I happier in Moon Ridge than I'd been when I lived in the dorms?

I'd been so caught up on being trapped and abducted and whatnot that I hadn't really thought about that.

Thinking back to my life, I remembered the simplicity of going to school, studying, working at the sandwich shop, and then repeating it all again. I'd only chatted with Ebony a little every day, and I had no other close friends other than my mom.

That, compared to a life where I did everything with Jesse, had someone to verbally spar with all the time, and was constantly being fed coffee and other food...

I swallowed roughly.

Holy shit.

My life as a werewolf—as a monster—was so damn much better than it had been when I was living back in my dorm room at college.

How had I not realized that earlier?

How had I not seen that?

Even before Jesse turned human, Wolf Jesse was always there listening to me, conversing with me in his weird wolfy way.

I'd been lonely living on campus, and over the past few months, I'd practically forgotten what that word meant.

I was never alone anymore.

And... I loved it.

And if Jesse really became my mate, I would never have to be alone again.

"Holy shit," I whispered. "I can't seriously be considering this. Accepting that I'm... a werewolf. And that I'm happy being a werewolf. That's huge."

It was huge. Insanely, ridiculously huge.

But I remembered what Jesse's mom had said. That she wouldn't trade anything for her werewolf life, and that she'd give it all up again for her mate.

I wasn't quite there yet, but suddenly, it didn't sound so ridiculous.

"Wow," I said out loud, to the car or the air or just to myself. "Am I losing my mind?"

I knew I probably was, but I didn't feel like I was losing my mind; I felt like I was finally starting to understand it.

I liked Jesse.

I *wanted* Jesse.

And I sure as hell had fun kissing him.

What if his wolf had chosen me for a reason? What if he'd somehow seen that I was lonely, that I needed him?

I still wasn't sure I felt comfortable being the one who cared more, but Ebony was right that it wasn't a competition. If Jesse didn't like kissing me, I'd figure out a better way to do it, because I was damn sure I liked kissing him.

And if he only liked me because we were mates... well, I'd give him more reasons to fall for me. I knew I was pricklier than a damn cactus, and that I was far from the most loving, kind person on the planet, but I would try.

Because I was pretty sure Jesse was worth it.

My thoughts kept moving all the way back to Moon Ridge. I parked in the garage, and Jesse was opening the front door as I stepped in through the garage one.

For the first time possibly ever, he looked pissed at me. "What the hell was that, Teapot?" He gestured to the car. "You went to a bar, and I know you're not twenty-one. Then you ditched me after I kissed you, and went out for sandwiches with the friend you've barely talked to in months? I'm getting really damn confused here."

"Why didn't you like it?" I ignored his questions, asking one of my own instead. His expression morphed to one of frustrated confusion. "The kiss. Why didn't you like kissing me? Am I too slobbery or something? Is my mouth too small? Or—"

"Why the *hell* would you think I didn't like kissing you?"

"You were hardly affected at all, afterward. I was panting like a freaking dog, and you just waved at a guy and moved me out of the way."

"We were blocking the road. That has nothing to do with whether or not I enjoyed it, Tea." He raked hair out of his eyes. "You're fucking gorgeous, and you tasted like whiskey, coffee, and that minty lip gloss you use like it's Chapstick. I'm getting horny just thinking about kissing you again." He gestured to his junk, which was hidden by his coat. "I'm sorry I was shitty at showing that I enjoyed it, but you were looking at me like I'd just murdered a small animal, and my first kiss had just turned into a wet-dream-worthy make out session, and we were blocking the damn road."

"I was looking at you like you'd murdered a small animal?" I asked incredulously.

"Why else would I have apologized?"

"Jesse." I shut my eyes, exhaling slowly before opening them back up. "I only looked like that because I was shocked. I've kissed a decent number of guys, and a kiss has never felt like that before."

"Like what?" His gaze was intense.

"Like I never want it to end. Like I'm burning, and I never want the fire to go out. Like—"

He cut me off by crossing the distance between us and taking me in his arms. His tongue parted my mouth, and he devoured me.

My arms locked around his neck, fingers finding his hair and shoulders as we kissed. He lifted me up off the ground, and I wrapped my legs around his hips.

Emotions burned through me as our lips and tongues danced, and he hauled me into the kitchen, setting me down on the island. With my ass on the cold countertops, it was easier to adjust my position against his erection.

I groaned as he pressed against me, hitting me in all the right places.

"Jesse." I tilted my head back, and his lips latched onto the sensitive skin beneath my ear. He sucked, and I arched into him.

He stopped. "Not good?"

"It's incredible. Just don't leave a hickey."

He sucked harder, and I smacked him halfheartedly on the side of the head.

"You heal much faster than a human now." He flashed me a devilish grin before his lips caught mine again. Our tongues fought again, longer, our hands starting to explore the dips and curves in each other's bodies.

But then my wolf interfered.

I cried out, my body arching backward as something in my spine cracked.

Why did the spine always go first?

"Easy," Jesse murmured, as his hand smoothed over my hair. He held me to his chest. "Stop fighting her. Let her have control."

I tried, I really did, but something inside me just couldn't help but fight the wolf. She wanted me out, and I wanted her out, and there was no peace between us.

A scream tore through the air as I bent further, and Jesse eased me off the counter. He sat on the floor with me in his arms, and spoke calming words as he quickly helped me out of my clothes. He wasn't exactly a professional at getting a woman undressed, so he barely finished in time.

My wolf took control, and the pain faded away.

Jesse tugged his shirt off his head, then stepped out of his jeans. I stared at him, drinking in the sight of the gorgeous man. He still wore underwear, but there was plenty to look at anyway.

"Have you decided where you'll bite me yet?" Jesse asked my wolf, sitting down on the floor. Those gorgeous legs of his sprawled out in front of him, and his body's response to our make out session was about a thousand percent obvious.

And I loved that he didn't try to hide that.

The wolf prowled in a circle around him. Jesse didn't come off as eager, but there was a gleam in his eyes that told me he was riling her up, the way he always riled me up.

She seemed to like it as much as I did.

"Legs are the most common places for men to wear mate bites," Jesse continued. "Followed by torso, then arms. I've seen a couple guys with gnarly neck bites, and one whose mate decided to mark his face. I could rock a neck bite, but I'd rather you not mar all this." He gestured to his face.

I cringed inwardly.

Please don't bite his neck or face, wolf.

She couldn't hear me, but it was worth the effort.

My wolf continued stalking around him, studying his body to figure out where exactly she wanted her mark on him.

He reached out to scratch her fur, and she was done deciding.

She lunged.

THIRTY-ONE

HER TEETH CLOSED around Jesse's wrist. His jaw clenched, but he watched my wolf intensely as she bit down on him. She wasn't trying to hurt him, the way she'd tried to hurt the girl on campus, so she didn't bite hard at all.

When she withdrew from his hand, she licked his wound. The fingers on his other hand tangled in her fur, and he tugged her against his chest.

"Thank you," he murmured to her. "I feel lucky that you chose me as your mate."

She licked his face, and he scratched behind her ears.

The wolf turned to his injury, licking at the blood until the wound stopped bleeding and closed up. It healed miraculously fast, and then the wolf snuggled up against Jesse. He stood up straight, lifting her and hauling her upstairs. "To bed with you," he told the wolf.

She whined.

"I know it's early, but it's been a long day. And you used your venom when you bit me, so I know you're feeling worn-out. Tea will need to do a lot of schoolwork tomorrow, so you've got to sleep when you can," he warned the wolf.

When he set her down on his bed, she dropped her head to her paws and stared at him.

Her stomach rumbled, and Jesse swore. "I haven't been feeding you enough."

She made a noise of agreement.

"I'll be right back with food." He disappeared back down the stairs.

As soon as he was gone, the wolf withdrew from me rapidly. I bit down on a groan as my body slowly shifted back over three or four minutes, and when I was me again, flopped to the bed on my stomach.

A wave of something tore through my lower belly, and I bit back a moan.

Was I feeling...horny?

Oh shit.

The Climax.

Jesse's footsteps were loud on the stairs. He held a giant plate of food, but stopped before stepping inside the room.

I peeked an eye at him, and saw his hand reach up to grip the doorway. He clutched the plate like it was a lifeline.

"Shit," he hissed.

Another wave of heat tore through my abdomen. I moaned, rolling over to my back to take the weight off of it.

"Dammit." His jaw was clenched tight. "Blanket on, now."

Good idea.

I grabbed it and tugged it over my skin, all the way up to my neck.

Jesse walked stiffly over to me. Since he was still only wearing his underwear, his bulge was obvious.

"Eat this," he said gruffly.

My horny, lust-driven mind took my eyes straight to his dick.

He swore again. "Teapot..."

"We might need a chaperone," I murmured.

His eyes flooded with hatred. "I'll kill anyone who comes near you."

Shit.

"How long does this last?"

"A couple of days, if we act on it." His eyes closed, his jaw clenching tightly.

"If we don't?"

"Weeks."

I grabbed a peanut butter sandwich off the loaded plate Jesse had brought me, hoping it would distract me from my body's urges. "What if you shift? Would that help?"

He laughed bitterly. "My wolf won't take over when I'm feeling like this."

"Like what, exactly?" I asked, wanting to hear the words.

"Like nothing on the damn planet matters except having you wrapped around my dick." He sat down on the edge of the bed.

I moaned again at his words, as the heat grew more intense. "How do we stop it?"

"Sex." He bent at the middle, his hands landing on his knees. "Dammit." He looked around for something.

"What?" I croaked, forcing myself to take another bite of the sandwich. My hand pressed into my lower belly, trying desperately hard to ignore the ache between my legs.

"My phone's downstairs. I need to call the guys to come over in case I do something stupid."

"Like join me under the blankets and kiss me?"

His eyes darkened. "Like rip the blankets off and lick every inch of your skin."

Another surge of heat made breathing a little more difficult. "What if we just... do it?"

He stared at me.

"You probably don't want your first time to be while we're in the climax, but there's no way it can be worse than my first time. And we've marked each other, so we're stuck together. That's permanent, right?"

His jaw clenched. "Tell me you're not messing with me."

"I'm not." I shoved the plate and my sandwich onto the bedside table, rolling slightly so I could see him better. "I don't want you to regret it, though."

"Regret making love with my mate while we're both horny as hell?" He barked out a laugh.

"Then get over here and kiss me." I lifted the blankets.

He ripped them off me completely, tossing them over to the side of the bed. "I'm not thinking straight," he warned me.

"Neither am I." I flashed him a devious grin. "That might make it more fun, though."

"Damn straight."

His hot gaze swept my figure quickly, and then slower. The burning in my lower belly returned, and I moved uncomfortably. Not because I was naked, but because I felt like I might combust.

"I want to taste you," Jesse growled, leaning over me on the bed. He positioned himself slightly to the side of me, sliding down my body so his gaze was almost level with my core before he slowly parted my legs. It felt weird to be open and exposed like that, but the way he stared at me made me feel sexy.

"Are you sure?" My throat felt swollen, suddenly, my body growing hotter just at the thought of it. The only time I'd had sex was awkward and painful; there hadn't been any foreplay, or touching, and there definitely hadn't been oral.

"Hell yes." He leaned over me, his hand catching on the curve of my hip and gripping me as he leaned over and pressed his lips to my abdomen.

A strangled cry escaped me.

Just seeing his face so close to me was making me so damn turned on I couldn't think straight.

He slowly trailed kisses down my lower belly. I squirmed a little, growing more desperate by the second.

Jesse spread my legs open further as he continued trailing his kisses downward, and I moaned as he brushed his thumb over my core. He found my clit in a in instant, giving it a slow rub before his tongue descended on me.

Guess being a virgin didn't mean he hadn't taken an anatomy lesson or two of his own.

His tongue was hot and wet, exploring me slowly at first. Noises I didn't know I could make started to escape me as the pressure built within me, and it seemed like he'd only just started when I shattered with a cry.

"Fuuck," he groaned into me, reaching for his cock.

More moans escaped me as I watched him pump his fist over his erection while his mouth and other hand continued working my core. He lost control, quickly, but only devoured me faster and more fiercely afterward.

"You're going to put that inside me, right?" I panted, so close to a second climax that my breathing was ragged.

He lifted his lips from my core, his eyes burning into mine.

Shit, I loved the way he looked between my thighs.

"Hell yeah. Just needed to get ready."

His tongue found my clit again as he slid a finger inside me for the first time. I cried out, my body arching at the touch, and he gripped my ass with his free hand as he held me spread wide.

Another finger joined the first, and I started to pant again.

He was big; he needed to stretch me out. And hot damn, I couldn't wait.

A third finger joined, and I was so close, so damn close to another orgasm, but he didn't give me time.

"Ready, Teapot?" He trailed his tongue off my core, down my inner-thigh. My whole body was over-sensitized already, and the sweep of his tongue made me cry out.

"Give it to me," I snarled at him.

His chuckle only made me burn hotter.

Slowly, so damn slowly, he settled himself over the top of me. The way our entire bodies pressed together was so insanely sensual, it nearly pushed me over the edge.

His hand found his cock, and he aligned it with my core. My lips parted, my head leaning back as he pushed into me slowly.

The feeling was alien, but so, so good.

He continued slowly making his way inside me, but I was so close—and I didn't want slow.

Tilting my hips, I pushed myself forward, wrapping my legs around him and dragging him deep inside me.

A tortured groan escaped him, and I cried out as he filled me.

And holy shit, I had not expected it to feel so *good*.

"Tea," he growled at me, chest heaving as he slowly moved within me. "You okay?"

"So okay," I moaned, grinding my hips to move him inside me.

We groaned again together, picking up speed as we moved. He started to thrust in and out, and pressure built inside me again with every movement. The friction was so, so good, but then he put his hand on my clit—and it was all over.

I came so hard that I lost control of myself. More new noises escaped me as I rode out the orgasm on his cock, this time. He snarled as he pumped into me, faster and faster, until he shattered with me.

We collapsed to the bed together, breathing hard and clutching each other fiercely tight.

"Holy shit," I panted, my hair wild and my heart pumping, but my heart feeling more light and alive than ever. "Jesse,"

"Teagan," he flashed me a grin, his chest rising and falling rapidly too. His hand smoothed over my hair, but only managed to mess it up further. "You're so damn sexy."

"Same." I closed my eyes, leaning my forehead against his chest as he laughed.

"Same? That's all I get?"

"If you want more words, you shouldn't get me off so many times," I mumbled.

"That's fair," he said, the humor evident in his voice.

His hand slid over the curve of my hip, moving slowly and seductively over my skin. My body slowly began to heat up, growing hotter, like it had when he was downstairs.

"Jesse," I whispered.

"Yeah?" His hand curved around my ass, squeezing and feeling. He had yet to stop touching me, and I wasn't sure he had any desire to do so.

"Are you starting to feel horny again?"

"Mmhmm. It's the climax. Our bodies won't give us much of a break. I need to feed you before we go again though."

I groaned. "Grab the food, then."

He chuckled, rolling me over so I was on top of him. Everything felt different like that—and I loved it.

"Here." He grabbed something off the plate, and when he put it to my lips, I smelled peanut butter. "Eat this."

"What if I want to eat something else?" I teased him.

His eyes flashed with heat. "We'll get there. Sandwich first."

With a laugh, I took a bite of the sandwich.

His hands ran over my skin as I ate, slipping between my thighs before the food was even halfway gone. I was panting before the damn thing was two-thirds gone, and he put the last bite of the sandwich in my mouth as I shattered on his fingers.

I moaned curses at him, struggling to swallow the food, which only made him grin.

And then devour me, again.

THIRTY-TWO

WE WERE four days into the Climax when someone finally interrupted us. Our sex drives were still high, but starting on day three, the constant need finally began to fade.

"We're going to starve," I groaned to Jesse, staring into the fridge. It was empty, other than a gallon of milk with less than a swallow of liquid left inside it, and our basic condiments. "We've legitimately eaten ourselves out of house and home."

I stood naked in the kitchen, my hair a mess and the rest of me just as wild. I'd missed my classes on Friday, and was hoping the Climax would be over in time for school on Monday... but at the same time, wasn't hoping for it to slow down at all.

Jesse sat on the countertop, also naked. I'd tried to convince him that it was gross to sit on the counter bare-assed, but that was two days earlier. And after we'd gotten freaky on the same counter, it seemed like a moot point.

We definitely needed to deep clean the entire house after the constant horniness faded, but it was so freakin' worth it. I'd never felt so calm, or so damn loved, in my entire life.

"I'll order food." He wrapped his arms around my shoulders. "Or I can call—"

The doorbell rang three times, and then about a dozen knocks followed.

I tilted my head to give Jesse a "WTF" look, and he jumped off the counter. "I'm sure it's the guys. Go grab some clothes." He kissed my head.

I'd have argued with him, but I knew his packmates—our packmates—had spare keys to our house. If we didn't answer, they'd probably come in anyway.

Jesse didn't open the front door until he heard me shut the one to our room. I looked around for a few minutes before realizing that my clothes were still in the room I'd decided was mine back before the Climax started.

After a solid face-palm, I slipped out into the hallway. I stopped when I heard Jesse talking, though.

"She's incredible. The best damn thing that ever happened to me." His voice was borderline-worshipping.

"That's a cool place for a bite," one of the guys said.

"Almost looks like a bracelet," another one agreed. They were teasing him, but Jesse was the perfect guy to tease because he loved to laugh and would always have a comeback.

I'd told him the same thing, and Jesse had said, "The coolest damn bracelet ever."

"Tease me all you want. I've got the sexiest woman alive in my bed, naked," Jesse said, his voice so proud that I was biting back a grin.

The guys continued making fun of each other while I slipped into the bedroom that held my clothes, and got dressed quickly.

"Teapot?" Jesse's voice was in the hallway. "Where'd you go?"

I stepped out of the bedroom wearing a long-sleeved top and a pair of skinny jeans. A strip of skin showed between my top and jeans, putting my mating bite on display. Jesse had become kind of obsessed with the marking, so I liked to make sure he could see it.

He covered the distance between us quickly, still naked—and getting hard again. "Damn. You look almost as good in clothes as you do out of them."

"Your friends are downstairs," I whispered, shooing him toward our room.

He grumbled. "They think we're doing dinner here today."

We hadn't been keeping up on time and shit; I had no idea it was even dinner time.

"Well it's probably our turn." I shrugged.

Stepping into the bathroom, I tugged a brush through my hair and then threw it up in a ponytail. Jesse leaned against the doorway, watching me swipe a little mascara on my lashes.

"You don't put on makeup for me," he remarked.

"I can if you want me to; I'm just lazy."

He considered it. "I like that you're confident looking natural around me."

"Me too." I stepped past him, going up on my tiptoes to kiss his lips. Leaning up to his ear after a slow, scorching kiss, I murmured, "The sooner they leave, the sooner we can take our clothes off again."

I paused. "And you should probably hurry to meet me downstairs. Some of these guys are probably going to be remembering the way I kissed them."

A soft snarl escaped him. Our lips collided, and he spoke against my mouth. "You're mine, Teapot."

"Keep telling yourself that, Kettle." I patted him on the shoulder, slipping away from him.

He caught my hips, his tongue snaking down my neck. He sucked my skin into his mouth and I bit back a groan, grinding my ass into his erection.

"You'd better be reminding *them* that." He swatted me on the butt before he strode into the bedroom, not bothering to shut the door behind himself.

I headed down the stairs, trying to remind myself that it hadn't been long since we'd last had sex. We were finishing up with the Climax, not just starting it. We could make it an hour without jumping each other's bones.

"Teagan," Rocco held his arms out toward me. "Welcome to the pack, permanently."

A smile parted my lips. "Thanks." I gave a fake bow. "I'm flattered to be a part of such an official group of kidnappers."

"Smartass." Rocco grinned at me.

"One of my best qualities," I agreed.

"What is?" Jesse asked, reaching the bottom of the stairs and wrapping his arms loosely around my middle. He'd thrown on sweats and a t-shirt, and I missed all that yummy bare skin.

"Her ass, according to Rocco," Zed called from the kitchen.

Jesse shot Rocco a death glare, and Rocco's hands lifted in surrender.

"They're messing with you, dummy." I patted him on the arm. "He called me smartass, and I told him it was one of my best qualities. There's no flirting happening here, so sit your possessive butt down and chill."

Jesse relaxed, dragging me toward the kitchen table.

"How long until Jesse quits with the caveman stuff?" I asked, gesturing behind me as my man sat me down on his lap at the kitchen table.

"He'll get less possessive the longer you're together, but if someone hits on you, the response won't ever really change." Elliot shrugged.

I made a face.

"It'll get easier when the rest of us are mated, because then he won't see us as a threat," Dax added.

Well, that was better than nothing. "How can we speed that up?" I checked. "And avoid kidnapping future mates?"

"There's no way around the kidnapping. We've been over this," Ford reminded me.

"We'll think of something," I brushed that right off.

"And there's no way to speed up finding our mates. If there was, we'd have already done it," Rocco said.

The room grew a bit quieter. My gaze swept the space.

Damn, they wanted their ladies.

"Well I hope one of you brought food, because our fridge is officially empty," I declared.

A few of the guys chuckled.

"We've got the goods," Rocco promised, though his typical grin wavered a bit. "Zed even offered to cook. He'll act like he's not glad you're here, but he's full of shit."

A few of the other guys grinned, and Jesse's chuckle rumbled my back.

"Is Zed a bad cook or something?" I looked between the guys.

"Or something," Zed scoffed.

"He's a chef at the fanciest restaurant in town," Elliot said, like a proud mom.

I was pretty sure he wouldn't appreciate the comparison, and kept it to myself.

"Damn," I whistled. "What do the rest of you do?"

They went around, telling me their jobs and college majors. They were all trying to get through their degrees as fast as possible, in preparation for meeting their mates. I thought it was really sweet.

Jesse was quiet behind/beneath me, but his hand stroked up and down my thigh pretty consistently. It was only slightly distracting.

Not as distracting as the erection pressed against my ass, though.

It was a good thing we had an entire extra day before I went back to school.

We chatted while Zed cooked, and much to my surprise, it was actually kind of fun. Jesse's packmates were cool to have around now that they weren't afraid I was going to kiss them again, and they seemed at least somewhat interested in me and my life.

Jesse remained fairly quiet, only contributing when someone asked him a question directly. I was pretty sure he was just trying to adapt to the new dynamic of being the only mated guy in the group, as well as trying to adjust to his possessive tendencies that probably made him feel like his friends were a threat sometimes.

After a delicious dinner in which I ate twice more than Rocco and the rest of them, they left us alone again.

As soon as they were gone, Jesse's hands were on my ass, his lips locked with mine. My back hit the front door, my legs winding around his waist.

A knock behind my head had us freezing in place.

"We heard a thud. Are you okay?" Elliot yelled through the door.

Totally the pack's mom.

"We're fine," Jesse yelled back, giving no explanation for the thud.

There was a long pause.

"Alright. Good night!" Elliot called out.

We waited a few minutes, our eyes meeting before we both burst out laughing. We laughed so hard that we cried, and then laughed some more.

"Shit," Jesse said with a grin, as he hauled me up the stairs. "I didn't think about them hearing."

"You win some and you lose some." I grinned back, wiping at my eyes with one hand and holding on to Jesse with the other, since he was still carrying me reverse-backpack style.

"Nah. I'm on a permanent winning-streak." Jesse kissed me, pinning me between him and our bedroom door since the front one was now off-limits for the time being. "At least with you." He caught my lips.

THIRTY-THREE

LATE THAT NIGHT—OR maybe early the next morning—Jesse and I were snuggling in his bed. We'd talked a ton over the last few days, but mostly about dreams and childhood stories and such. We hadn't actually had a discussion about the present, which was probably not great, but it wasn't like we were running out of time. Our wolves had paired us together, and there was no escaping that.

"So I know you're majoring in Software Engineering, unless my research was wrong," I told him.

He chuckled softly. "Your research was right."

"I've never asked you about it. Why are you doing it? How did you make all the money in that damned envelope you gave me? How much longer do you have before you graduate?" I fired off questions at him.

His fingers stroked my back lazily, just enjoying the feel of my skin while I enjoyed the feel of his touch.

"I was only two weeks into my final semester when I met you. Our packmates withdrew me from my courses, so I've still got just that final semester left," he said. "I'll probably start back up in January, and finish in May."

"Wow. Sorry I interrupted your last semester."

"Don't be. You're more important—and more fun." He tickled my side, which he knew was ticklish.

I shrieked and squirmed, smacking him on the chest when he finally stopped. "Damn you," I complained halfheartedly.

"Damn me," he agreed, a smile playing on his lips. "As to the rest of your questions, I'm studying software engineering because I like computers. I've been fixing people's computers and teaching the older werewolves in Moon Ridge how to use them ever since I was a teenager. That's how I saved up the money," he explained. "The jobs got tougher, but also started to pay more, as I learned more. Now, I'm a freelance software engineer. I work when I want to, and don't when I don't. I'll make more when I graduate; a company in town already offered to hire me. Assuming you can get a nursing job here, I'd like to stick around."

The Climax high faded a bit.

I'd always wanted to live by my mom. It had been a plan since I was a teenager—one I wasn't sure I could let go of.

"Do we have to stay by the pack?" I asked finally.

"No. I'd like to, though," he admitted.

I bit my lip.

"We could see if your mom wants to move here," Jesse suggested. I guess he knew where my mind had gone.

"To a werewolf city?" I lifted an eyebrow at him.

"Sure. You could tell her what you are, if you want. What we are. A lot of humans do it, and a decent number of them live here in town."

I nodded slowly. "I'll think about it."

I would. I wasn't going to give up my dream of living by her, but Jesse and I could talk about it. I could understand a werewolf's desire to stay by their pack, and I was starting to feel the same way, though I wasn't quite there yet.

On Monday, sadly I had to return to school. I was behind on my studying, but I had gotten all my actual assignments turned in, so that was something. And after my five days off, I felt rejuvenated.

Jesse picked up a few clients after I told him he didn't need to go sit in my classes with me anymore, and he seemed a bit excited to get back into his work. I liked that he enjoyed what he did. It made me feel better about pursuing what I wanted to do, too.

The whole school was buzzing about the wolf attack, which made me feel like shit all over again, but Jesse and the rest of the pack kept promising me that my possessiveness was normal and that it was something I would just learn how to live with.

The semester ended a few weeks later, and Jesse and I got in the car to go visit my mom for Christmas. We'd done a small celebration with his family before we left, and they had their own pack to celebrate with, so they didn't seem to mind us leaving.

After a few hours on the road, we parked in front of my mom's place. I'd decided shortly after mine and Jesse's conversation that I'd tell her I was a werewolf—and that I'd ask her if she wanted to move to Moon Ridge or a city near it after her school year ended, since I was going to be staying there. Sometimes I still felt like a monster, but living in Moon Ridge, it was nice to know that I wasn't the only one.

"Ready?" I asked Jesse.

"Sure am." He laced his fingers through mine. "Hopefully she doesn't drool when I tell her my favorite thing to do is work out."

I swatted him on the arm, though I couldn't help but grin. "Shut up." I rang the doorbell, knowing the door was locked.

"Make me," he taunted.

I went up on my tiptoes and pressed my lips to his.

My mom chose that moment to open the door.

"Oh my," she exclaimed.

I jerked away from Jesse. She knew I was dating him, but didn't know how serious we were.

And I *may* have forgotten to mention bringing him home for Christmas.

"Hi, mom," I cringed.

"This is Jesse, then," she looked him up and down, then looked at me with raised eyebrows.

"I know what you're thinking, if you're anything like your daughter. And the answer is no, I'm not a football player." Jesse cracked a grin, holding his hand out. "Hi."

"Hello." She shook his hand awkwardly, then gestured both of us inside. As I passed her, she grabbed my arm. He let go of my hand, walking inside and pretending to check the place out to give us a moment of privacy. "You didn't tell me you were serious enough to bring him home," she whispered. "A warning would've been nice."

"I know. I'm sorry." I gave her an apologetic grimace. "There's a lot I haven't told you this semester. Can we sit down?"

My mom looked uncertain, but nodded.

Jesse and I sat down on the couch across from her, and told her everything that had happened that semester (minus the copious amount of sex). And then, we showed her what we were.

I didn't expect her immediate acceptance, but if she disapproved, she didn't voice it.

Instead, she embraced us both, and said she would most certainly move to Moon Ridge... when she was good and ready.

And that was good enough for me.

EPILOGUE

A FEW WEEKS after school started again, I met up with Ebony on a Wednesday evening. We'd kept up with the tradition, though sometimes our little dinners were fairly short. It was hard to talk to her without telling her about the werewolf part of my life, but it was better than not talking to her at all.

She showed up looking a bit frazzled—and she never looked frazzled.

"Tea." She gestured me toward a table.

I glanced at the sandwich line, my stomach rumbling. Jesse was meeting me there after he got off work, so we could eat dinner together. It was going to be a second dinner for me, but second dinner had become necessary. Often, third dinner too.

Giving it a sad look, I sat down across from Ebony.

"What's up?" I asked. We usually didn't beat around the bush before getting food and shoving it down our gullets. Now that I had a sugar daddy, I could afford to eat out once or twice a week. I still felt shitty about accepting Jesse's money, but I was working through that, and we'd agreed that if we were going to be mated, we were going to share a bank account.

And he was really damn good at reminding me that buying me food was the least he could do for turning me into a constantly-hungry werewolf.

"I saw this video, from last semester," she said. There were dark circles under her eyes, and her gaze was stricken. She held her phone out to me, and showed me the video—the one where Jesse had shifted.

"Isn't that your dog?" she asked. Her dark skin was ashen, and her expression told me she already knew the answer.

"It is," I confirmed.

She fast forwarded a few seconds, to the part where Jesse's bare ass showed as he talked sense into my wolf. "And isn't that your roommate?" she pointed to his ass.

My wolf threatened to surge, and I took slow breaths to try to calm her. We'd started figuring out how to live together a bit more peacefully. It was slow-going, given that we couldn't communicate, but it was progress.

"It's hard to say, really," I tried to lie to her, but I could see in her eyes that she wasn't going to believe anything I said.

Her voice lowered. "There's only one possibility here, Tea. He's a werewolf. Your friend, roommate, boyfriend... he's a werewolf."

I forced a laugh. "That's crazy. Werewolves don't exist."

"I know, I know it sounds crazy, but my friend's a videographer and he thinks the video is legit. And if it's legit, that's the only logical explanation. He's a werewolf."

The door to the sub shop opened, and Jesse came strolling in with Ford and Rocco.

He was early.

Shit.

"Hey, Teapot," Jesse walked over, bending down to kiss my temple. "Hey, Ebony." He nodded at my friend.

She looked like she was going to hyperventilate, or pass out or something.

"You okay there, pretty—" Ford halted as his eyes collided with Ebony's. Then, they shifted to red.

My heart dropped into my stomach.

I knew exactly what he was going to say next.

"Mate."

Jesse and Rocco grabbed Ford, shoving him back out the door. Ebony looked at me, panic engraved in every line of her face. "His eyes changed! You can't tell me he's not one of them!"

I slid her arm over my shoulder to keep her upright, since she looked dangerously close to fainting.

"He's a werewolf. All of us are. I've got a lot to tell you." I led her out to Ford's car, where Jesse and Rocco were shoving a snarling, shifting Ford into the back seat. "You're going to have to come with us," I apologized. "After we talk, you can go home. But there's a lot to talk about."

I set her in the passenger seat, walking around to the driver's side. Jesse tossed me the keys, and I slipped into the driver's seat as the guys slammed the doors, squishing into the back on both sides of Ford.

Ebony was staring at the shifting man like he was going to eat her, and not in the fun way.

"He won't hurt you," I promised. "You're his mate; he can't. I learned that firsthand."

I pulled away from the shop, my stomach still growling as my gaze met Jesse's in the rearview mirror.

He gave me a small smile, and I returned it.

At least we didn't have to kidnap her.

The story continues every week in kindle vella here
Or read with kindle unlimited here

AFTERTHOUGHTS

I had so much fun writing this book. I laughed so many times, and I hope you did too! I shared a lot of my thoughts about the book as I was writing it on Kindle Vella, so I'm not going to rehash everything now, but I love this book so hard.

If you want me to continue writing standalones in this world, and standalones in general, please, please, PLEASE consider preordering book two and/or reading, liking, or following as I write Ebony's story on Kindle Vella. The success of this book and the second one on Vella will determine how many Mate Hunt standalones I write, because ultimately I have to write what sells.

Here's the link again if you want to follow along, and even if you don't, thank you so, so much for reading!

-Lola Glass

BONUS EPILOGUE

Join my mailing list with this link to read a bonus epilogue. It's not a necessary part of the story, but if you want a glimpse at a cute moment in these character's future, just put your email address in.
BONUS EPILOGUE
You'll receive a monthly update on my books as well as any upcoming deals and promotions. No spam!

PLEASE REVIEW

Here it is. The awkward page at the end of the book where the author begs you to leave a review.
Believe me, I hate it more than you do.
But, this is me swallowing my pride and asking.
Whether you loved or hated this story, you made it this far, so please review! Your reviews play a MASSIVE role in determining whether others read my books, and ultimately, writing is a job for me—even if it's the best job ever—so I write what people are reading.
Regardless of whether you do or not, thank you so much for reading <3
-Lola

ALSO BY LOLA GLASS:

Moon of the Monsters Trilogy

Sacrificed to the Fae King Trilogy

Shifter Queen Trilogy

Rejected Mate Refuge Trilogy & Standalones

Mate Hunt Standalones (Kindle Vella)

Mate Hunt Standalones (Kindle Unlimited)

<u>Wolfsbane Series</u>

Supernatural Underworld Duology

SAY HI!

Check out my reader group, Lola's Book Lovers
for giveaways, book recommendations, and more!

Or find me on:
INSTAGRAM
PINTEREST
GOODREADS

ABOUT THE AUTHOR

Lola is a book-lover with a *slight* werewolf obsession and a passion for love—real love. Not the flowers-and-chocolates kind of love, but the kind where two people build a relationship strong enough to last. That's the kind of relationship she loves to read about, and the kind she tries to portray in her books.

Even if they're about shifters :)

www.ingramcontent.com/pod-product-compliance
Ingram Content Group UK Ltd.
Pitfield, Milton Keynes, MK11 3LW, UK
UKHW050715100425
5418UKWH00021B/587